THE DEADLY
HUNTER

JEDI APPRENTICE

. . . and more to come

STAR WARS

JEDI APPRENTICE

The Deadly Hunter

Jude Watson

LUCAS BOOKS

SCHOLASTIC INC.

New York Toronto London Auckland Sydney
Mexico City New Delhi Hong Kong

ISBN 0-439-13930-9

12 11 10 9 8 7   3 4 5 6/0

Printed in the U.S.A.
First Scholastic printing, December 2000

*Heartfelt thanks to Jane Mason and
Sarah Hines Stephens for their
contribution to Jedi Apprentice.*

CHAPTER 1

Obi-Wan Kenobi slung his survival pack over his shoulder and yawned. It had been a long journey.

Around him rose the many levels of Coruscant, the city that covered a planet. He was standing on a landing platform at one of the high levels of the city, surrounded by tall buildings with spires and turrets. The mists around him could be atmosphere or clouds. The sky was filled with transports, large and small, that negotiated the air lanes with skill and daring.

Obi-Wan watched as his Master, the Jedi Knight Qui-Gon Jinn, thanked the space hauler pilot who had let them hitch a ride to Coruscant. He noted the respectful way Qui-Gon bowed to the scruffy creature. His manner was gentle, yet strength was behind every word and gesture. Obi-Wan hoped that one day he would have his Master's grace and assurance with other living beings. Often he just felt awkward with the many characters they met on their journeys.

Time passes and it teaches, Qui-Gon had told him. *You are fourteen. You have much to see and much to experience. Do not hurry the knowledge you seek. It takes its own time.*

"Sorry I can't bring you all the way," the pilot said to the Jedi. "But there are plenty of air taxis cruising this neighborhood."

"We are grateful for your help. I wish you a safe journey home," Qui-Gon said in his quiet way.

"Always glad to help out the Jedi," the pilot answered, giving them a cheerful wave.

Qui-Gon slung his survival pack over his shoulder and gave a satisfied look around. "It is good to be back," he said.

Obi-Wan nodded. Coruscant was where the Jedi Temple was located, and the Temple was home. It was almost time for the midday meal, and Obi-Wan had been thinking about it as the kilometers went by. He and Qui-Gon had been traveling throughout the galaxy for some time.

"Look, here comes an air taxi." Obi-Wan started forward.

"Wait, Padawan."

Obi-Wan turned. Qui-Gon hesitated and waved him back. "I have another idea. Would you mind if we made a stop first?"

Obi-Wan tried to hide his disappointment. "Whatever you wish."

Qui-Gon smiled. "It won't take long. There's someone I'd like you to meet — a friend. It's not far. We can walk there."

Qui-Gon strode to the end of the landing platform and activated a temporary crossing bridge to the next level. Here in the Senate district, the buildings were close together and the walkways were easy to navigate without relying on air transport.

Obi-Wan caught up to Qui-Gon's long stride. He waited, knowing that if Qui-Gon wanted to give him more information about this friend, he would.

"Didi Oddo runs a café near the Senate building," Qui-Gon explained. "He's an informant, of sorts. Many Jedi come to him for information. We don't pay him, but we try to watch out for him in return for his help. He knows all types on Coruscant — from Senatorial aides to gamblers to various beings who find laws a hindrance to their . . . operations." Qui-Gon gave a brief smile. "Everyone knows Didi's Café. I first met him when I was only a bit older than you are now."

Obi-Wan detected fondness in Qui-Gon's tone. His tiredness lifted. It would be interesting to meet a friend of Qui-Gon's. And a café meant he might be able to have a meal.

They traveled along a pedestrian walkway past shops and restaurants, all catering to the tourists and business people who traveled to Coruscant to either tour the Senate or offer petitions there. Occasionally they would have to activate a pedestrian bridge to move from one level to another. The walkways were crowded with beings from all over the galaxy. Talk bubbled around them in Basic as well as several languages unfamiliar to Obi-Wan.

Qui-Gon stopped before a small café on a corner. It appeared shabby beside the grander restaurants next door. An attempt had been made to improve it by painting the windowsills and doorframe a cheerful shade of blue. But the fresh coats of paint only made the cracked and pitted stone walls appear more run-down than they were.

Still, Obi-Wan noticed that the restaurant next door was empty, and the dingy café was packed. He could see everyone inside, sitting at small tables crowded together, all talking, gesturing, and eating enormous plates of food.

"Do not engage with anyone," Qui-Gon instructed him. "There are all types here, and fights are common."

He started for the entrance, then stopped and turned. "Oh, and one more thing. Whatever you do, don't eat the food."

Suppressing a sigh, Obi-Wan followed Qui-Gon into the bustling café. Tables were packed so closely together they could barely squeeze through. Obi-Wan nearly knocked one customer's plate to the floor. The customer, a Togorian, grabbed at it, snarling.

"Clumsy fool!"

Obi-Wan kept walking, carefully following Qui-Gon's graceful threading through the narrow spaces. Finally, they reached an open area near the back. A long bar ran along one wall. It was crowded with customers.

"That's enough for you there, Andoran," a cheerful voice called. "Finish your ale and get a plate of food to eat. You need food, not drink, my good friend. Pilus, do you call this a tip? You just made a fortune running spice to the Quintus system. You can do better — manys the favor I've done for you, and I have a daughter to raise. Nadarr, let me refill your tea. No, no, don't pay me, save it for your wife's care. Funny how we all get better when we can afford to pay the doctor."

Qui-Gon grinned. "That's Didi."

Obi-Wan still couldn't see anything. Then a small, round man with a melancholy face jumped onto a stool behind the bar. He reached up to grab a bottle, then turned and saw them.

"Stars and planets, it's Qui-Gon Jinn! Clear

the way, friends, I have a greeting to bestow!" The mournful face creased into a smile. With surprising agility, Didi leaped onto the bar, then onto the floor.

He threw his short arms around the tall Jedi. Obi-Wan stepped back, confused. He had never seen anyone hug Qui-Gon. The Jedi was such a private man that Obi-Wan expected him to disengage himself from the embrace. Instead, he pounded Didi on the back.

"It is good to see you," Qui-Gon said.

Didi released Qui-Gon. "You rogue, you stayed away too long. But my eyes thank me as they look upon your person."

Qui-Gon gestured at the café. "There have been changes. You've dressed up the place. New paint, new decoration. It looks nicer." He cast an eye along the food bar. "And cleaner."

Cleaner? Obi-Wan thought. *You mean it looked worse than this?*

"My daughter Astri's doing." Didi shrugged his round shoulders. "She's trying to attract a better clientele. Wants me to get rid of tables, have more elbowroom. Buy new plates . . . do renovations. She's even taken cooking lessons! She'll either ruin me or make me a fortune; I haven't decided which. And who is this delightful young man with you?"

"This is my Padawan, Obi-Wan Kenobi," Qui-Gon said.

Obi-Wan nodded at Didi. "I'm happy to meet you."

"And I you." Didi's face turned serious. He touched Qui-Gon's arm. "I think fate sent you to my door, my good friend."

Qui-Gon shot him a keen glance. "Is everything all right?"

"Everything is . . ." Didi paused. "We can't talk here. Come into the office."

Obi-Wan followed behind as Didi slid the panel open and ushered them into a cluttered back room. Supply boxes were stacked to the ceiling, and the desk was littered with account records, folded napkins, and a food-spattered apron.

As soon as the door swung shut behind them, Didi's cheerful face crumpled. He rubbed his plump hands together and fixed Qui-Gon with a mournful gaze.

"My friend," he said, "I am afraid. Danger stalks me. I need your help."

CHAPTER 2

"Tell me," Qui-Gon said. "You know I will help if I can."

Didi took a deep breath. "Only two days ago, I was almost kidnapped. I was simply walking down the street when a woman wearing plastoid armor came at me from behind on a swoop. Some sort of whip wrapped around my body and I was yanked toward her. Luckily a Cavrilhu happened to be standing near. He didn't like the fact that she knocked off his visor as she passed. He gave chase with a rather large vibroblade and she had to abandon her attempt. She left him with a lashing to remember her by."

"Who was she?" Qui-Gon asked.

"A bounty hunter," Didi said in a whisper. "I asked around. Nobody can be in this sector without information getting back to me. No one knows her home planet, but she's humanoid."

Qui-Gon received this news with dismay. Didi

had always managed to stay on the right side of the law — barely. Qui-Gon gave his friend a piercing look. "A bounty hunter? Why is she after you?"

"It was not me, I swear," Didi said fervently. "I may feed, let us say, some dubious creatures in the underworld, but I am no criminal. You know this, my friend. All right, all right," he said before Qui-Gon could speak, "perhaps I have once or twice bought my provisions on the black market. Maybe I've made a gambling bet or two. That doesn't mean I break laws."

Qui-Gon sighed. "It is against your best interest to gamble in such a way on Coruscant, Didi."

"Of course it is! How well I know that!" Didi cried, bobbing his head furiously in agreement. "But I'm convinced the bounty hunter is not after me. No doubt some government on another world has confused me for someone else. It happens, you know."

Qui-Gon saw the disbelief on Obi-Wan's face. He knew that his Padawan did not approve of Didi. He had not seen Didi's generous heart, the way he took care of the many beings who crowded his café without letting them know it. One of the lessons Obi-Wan needed to learn was to look beneath the surface. Perhaps this was one way.

"What would you like me to do, Didi?" Qui-Gon asked.

"Talk to her and tell her that there's been a mistake. Convince her that I'm innocent," Didi said earnestly.

"How would I find her?" Qui-Gon asked.

Obi-Wan shot him an incredulous look. Qui-Gon answered him with a glance that spoke as clearly as words. *Wait, Padawan.*

"I know where she is staying. An inn not far from here," Didi said rapidly. "You could go right now. For a Jedi, this is a tiny favor. It will take five minutes of your time. So easy for one as wise and strong as yourself. She cannot ignore a Jedi. You know how I love your person, Qui-Gon. I would never endanger you. Your life must be long, for I value you so."

Qui-Gon's eyes twinkled. "Ah, I see. I must live a long life for *your* sake, Didi."

"Ha! And you are so clever, too. Jedi wisdom, it catches me every time! Of course I didn't mean you should live long for me only," Didi said hurriedly. "So many depend on you. Like your Padawan here. Is that not right, Obi-Wan?"

Obi-Wan did not look pleased to be dragged into Didi's coaxing. "Excuse me, Didi," he said. "But if you're innocent of any charge, why can't you see the bounty hunter yourself? Ask her to do a retinal scan or check your identification papers. The matter can be cleared up in seconds."

"That would be a very good plan, were I not such a cowardly person," Didi told Obi-Wan earnestly. He turned back to Qui-Gon. "You see how he worships you. Just as I do. You question my love for you, and it hurts me." Didi dabbed at his dry eyes with a napkin he swooped up from a stack on the desk.

"All right, Didi," Qui-Gon said, bemused. "You can stop all this drama. I will see your bounty hunter."

Didi beamed. "She is at the Soft Landings Inn. It's in the third Senate Quadrant on Quarter Moon Street."

"We'll return shortly," Qui-Gon said. "Try not to get into any more trouble while we're gone."

"I will remain here and be very good," Didi assured him.

The Jedi quickly made their way through the crowded café and reached the street.

"I don't understand," Obi-Wan burst out as soon as they were in the open air. "Why do you trust him? What if Didi actually *did* commit a crime and he's using you to get the bounty hunter off his trail? His story doesn't make sense to me. Bounty hunters can be unprincipled, but they rarely make mistakes. Why did you agree?"

"Didi might seem disreputable to you, but I've never known him to lie," Qui-Gon answered calmly. "And he's right — he knows all the criminals on Coruscant, but he's not one himself."

"Master, it is not for me to question your decision," Obi-Wan said. "But it seems to me that you are involving us in something that is bound to be dangerous and is none of the Jedi's concern. Here is a man who seeks out criminals and the dregs of the galaxy in order to get information, which he then sells to the highest bidder. If you live in that sort of world, you deserve whatever bad luck comes your way."

"Perhaps," Qui-Gon said.

"I don't understand why you're helping him," Obi-Wan said, frustrated.

Qui-Gon hesitated. Then he said, "It's because he is my friend."

CHAPTER 3

"This place doesn't look as if it provides a soft landing to me," Obi-Wan observed, casting a dubious eye at the Soft Landings Inn. "More like a full-scale crash."

"I've seen many places such as this," Qui-Gon said. "It is a place for space travelers to get a few hours of sleep. It's not arranged for comfort."

The building was made from salvaged materials — durasteel sheets and conductor pipes that wrapped around the building as though they were strangling it to a last gasp. The entire structure leaned to one side. It looked as if a small push could knock it over. The stairs leading up to a battered durasteel door were lined with overflowing garbage bins.

"Well," Qui-Gon said philosophically, "we might as well get this over with."

They mounted the stairs and pressed a button to access the door. A voice came from a speaker mounted next to the frame.

"*Na hti vel*?"

"Visiting a guest," Qui-Gon said.

The door slid open. A small Togorian female shuffled out.

"We're looking for a woman," Qui-Gon said. "She's humanoid and wears a plastoid armor plate —"

"Third level. Number two." The Togorian swiveled to return to her room.

"What's her name?"

The Togorian didn't turn. "Who cares? Pays in advance."

Qui-Gon lifted an eyebrow at Obi-Wan. Obviously, the Soft Landings Inn didn't worry about security.

They hurried up the creaking stairs to the third level. Qui-Gon knocked on the door marked 2. There was no answer.

"I am Qui-Gon Jinn, a Jedi Knight," Qui-Gon called through the door. "We mean you no harm. We just wish to ask you some questions. I respectfully request permission to enter."

Again, there was no answer. But after a moment, the door slowly slid open. Obi-Wan sensed a slither of movement near the floor, but no other disturbance. The door seemed to have opened on its own. It was dark inside the room, and he could not see anyone. He felt danger shimmer out at him like cracks in broken transparisteel.

Qui-Gon must have felt the warning as well. Yet he walked boldly into the room without drawing his lightsaber. Obi-Wan did the same.

Qui-Gon headed directly to a window. He tilted the shade and pale yellow light filtered in.

The bounty hunter sat facing them on a stool, her back against the wall. Her shaved head picked up the light and gleamed like a pale moon. Her dark eyes studied her visitors without interest. Underneath the plastoid chest plate and thigh-high boots, her body was powerful and strong. When she stood, she would be close to Qui-Gon's height.

"We come on behalf of Didi Oddo," Qui-Gon said politely. "You are trying to capture him, yet he has done no wrong. He requests that you check your information or contact the government or party that has sent you. He is sure that you have located the wrong person. Will you do this?"

The bounty hunter said nothing. Her eyes stayed on Qui-Gon, but they were expressionless.

"Didi Oddo runs a café," Qui-Gon said. "He is not a criminal. He rarely leaves Coruscant."

Silence.

"If you would allow me to check the warrant, I could clear this up immediately," Qui-Gon said. "Then we could be on our way."

More silence. Obi-Wan forced himself to remain still. He knew better than to fidget. This was a contest of wills. Qui-Gon stood easily, the same polite expression on his face. He would not show the bounty hunter that she had intimidated him with her silence. No one intimidated Qui-Gon.

"I'm afraid I must insist," Qui-Gon said, his voice hardening a fraction. "If a wrong has occurred, we should check it immediately. You would want the same."

Again, the bounty hunter did not reply. She appeared bored by her visitors. Or maybe she slept with her eyes open . . .

The movement came out of nowhere, taking him by surprise. He had been watching her face in order to determine what she would do. She barely moved a muscle, but with a casual flick of her fingers a whip arched into the air, its spiked tip heading straight for his face.

Obi-Wan backed up, but the whip curled around his neck several times. It tightened as he clawed at it.

Qui-Gon's extraordinarily fast reflexes were sharper than Padawan's. His lightsaber activated in a blur of light. He sprang forward to slash at the whip in order to sever it.

But the bounty hunter's agile fingers flicked again, and the whip reversed its twist and uncoiled off Obi-Wan's neck. It was just out of the lightsaber's reach, taunting Qui-Gon's blade.

The bounty hunter sprang to her feet. The whip flashed again, this time wrapping around Obi-Wan's ankles as he stepped forward to attack.

Obi-Wan stumbled and had to break his fall with one hand. Heat blazed in his face. He hated being clumsy. This was the second time the bounty hunter had surprised him. Fury clouded his vision for a moment, and he had trouble focusing on the calmness he would need for the battle.

The whip retracted. Suddenly, it glowed red in the dim room. It had been turned to laser mode.

Qui-Gon's lightsaber tangled with the whip. Smoke rose as the two lasers buzzed. Even while entangled with the lightsaber, the bounty hunter manipulated the end of the whip so that it slashed at Qui-Gon's forearm. Qui-Gon was forced to retreat and come at his opponent from another direction.

Obi-Wan leaped forward to help him, already

flexing so that he could come at her with a reverse backhand sweep. She flipped backward three times to avoid him, then dropped unexpectedly to the floor and rolled in a ball back to the window. Her movements were liquid, as though she were boneless. Obi-Wan had never seen such acrobatic skill.

The window was open a few centimeters at the bottom. To Obi-Wan's astonishment, the bounty hunter shed her armor and flattened herself enough to slip through the small opening like water, pulling the armor behind her. In another moment, she was gone.

Qui-Gon deactivated his lightsaber. He stood staring after the bounty hunter. "A formidable opponent."

"How did she do that?" Obi-Wan asked.

"At least now we know where she is from," Qui-Gon said, shutting down his lightsaber. "The planet Sorrus. Sorrusians have a skeletal system that can compress, allowing them to squeeze through tight places. She is remarkably flexible. Not to mention very good with a whip."

Obi-Wan touched his neck. "She certainly knows how to use it."

"I've never seen that weapon before," Qui-Gon mused. "It has two modes, one a laser. She was remarkably fast, Padawan. Don't question yourself. Your reflexes will get faster as you gain more control of the Force."

"You were already moving when I was strangling," Obi-Wan said ruefully.

"I was expecting the whip," Qui-Gon said. "Didi told us about it. I was watching her wrist. Next time, you will be as well."

Qui-Gon twisted around to look at his shoulder. Obi-Wan saw that his tunic was tattered. Blood soaked the edges. "You're hurt!"

"The spikes caught me. A little bacta and I'll be fine. Come, Padawan. We'd better get back to Didi with the bad news." Qui-Gon grimaced as he peeled back the cloth from the wound. "I don't think this bounty hunter is going away."

CHAPTER 4

"She injured your person!" Didi cried as soon as he saw Qui-Gon. "I cannot believe such a thing!" His hands flew to his mouth. "That means she is truly dangerous. Oh, I am in more trouble than I thought!"

"Never mind your troubles for the moment. We need water so we can clean the wound," Obi-Wan said sharply to Didi.

"Of course, of course, let me help. I have a med kit here somewhere . . ." Didi began to fuss around the desk, pushing aside datasheets, receipts, tins, and boxes.

"Never mind. Obi-Wan, it is okay to leave me. Go get your medpac," Qui-Gon said.

Quickly, Obi-Wan found his medpac. Didi brought a basin of water. Obi-Wan moved forward but Didi waved him away.

Obi-Wan watched as Didi cut away the tunic and carefully cleaned the wound, making sure no dirt or fabric remained in the torn flesh. His plump fingers were surprisingly delicate. He worked quickly and expertly, with no trace of hesitation. Obi-Wan couldn't help but admire his skill. He would have expected the excitable Didi to feel faint, or moan with sickness at the sight of blood.

Didi dripped bacta into the wound and then with great gentleness wrapped a clean bandage around it.

"Thank you," Qui-Gon said. "I could not ask for better care."

"You'll need a fresh tunic," Obi-Wan said.

"I can fetch one —" Didi began.

"In a moment." Qui-Gon frowned at Didi. "This bounty hunter is not giving up. Either she is very stubborn, or there truly is a warrant out for your arrest."

"Impossible," Didi said, shaking his head.

"Or there could be no warrant at all, just someone who wants to do Didi harm," Obi-Wan pointed out. "Bounty hunters often take private commissions."

Didi swiveled and stared at Obi-Wan, his mouth open. "Oh, do not say that, Obi-Wan. That is even worse. It would mean that someone has placed a death mark on my head."

Obi-Wan was taken aback at the sight of Didi's pale face. "I didn't mean to scare you."

"I appreciate that very much, dear boy," Didi said. "Very kind of you. But you did. Why would someone do such a thing? I have no enemies. Only friends."

"Obi-Wan, you make a good point," Qui-Gon said thoughtfully. "We should have considered this before. It is logical, considering the bounty hunter's attitude and how Didi makes his living."

"Serving food and drink?" Didi asked, baffled. "I admit some have gotten sick after supper, but I've never actually poisoned anyone. At least, not on purpose."

"I am not talking about your dubious cooking skills," Qui-Gon said to Didi. "I'm talking about your sideline. You traffic in information. Information that could benefit or harm criminals as well as security forces and members of the Senate. What if you know something that someone doesn't want to get out?"

"But what could it be?" Didi asked. "I don't know *anything*."

"You must," Qui-Gon insisted. "You just don't know what it is."

"How can I know something without knowing it?" Didi cried in frustration. "Is this worth a death sentence, I ask you? I hear something and pass it along for a tiny profit, and suddenly I am dead? Is that fair?"

Didi would have gone on, but Qui-Gon silenced him with an impatient gesture. "Let me see if we can narrow this down. If we knew who hired the bounty hunter, we could begin to investigate. Let me contact Tahl."

Didi slumped in a chair. Obi-Wan drew closer to Qui-Gon. "You're going to involve the Temple resources?" he asked in a low tone.

"Tahl is a friend of Didi's, too," Qui-Gon said, activating his comlink. "She'll want to help."

Seconds later, Obi-Wan heard Tahl's crisp voice over the comlink. After Qui-Gon filled her in on the situation, she said, "Didi is in trouble? Of course I want to help."

"I know the bounty hunter is Sorrusian," Qui-Gon said. "She didn't speak. She's about my size, and very muscular. She wears plastoid armor and has a shaved head."

"I know of her," Tahl said. "I don't know her name. Nobody does. We've received reports that are somewhat alarming, so Yoda asked me to keep track of her movements. It's hard because she tends to disappear into thin air. I didn't know she was on Coruscant. She doesn't work for governments, just private individuals with great wealth. She gained her reputation with a series of for-hire killings. Some of her victims have been in high-level government or finance."

"In other words," Qui-Gon said grimly, "she is able to get around high-level security."

"Exactly. And word is that she will take any assignment if the price is right. She's very good, Qui-Gon. Very dangerous."

A moan came from the desk.

Tahl's warm laugh came through the comlink. "I hear you, Didi. Do not fret. With Qui-Gon helping you, everything will turn out fine. Qui-Gon, I will see you and Obi-Wan soon, I'm sure. Yoda is expecting you shortly."

Tahl's voice was warm as she spoke to Didi. Obi-Wan didn't understand. Obviously, he missed whatever charms Didi had for the other Jedi.

Qui-Gon cut the communication. "The situation is getting interesting," he observed.

"I would hardly use that word," Didi said mournfully. "Terrifying, maybe. Horrible. Unfair. Hopeless —"

"The question is," Qui-Gon interrupted, ignoring Didi, "why would such a high-priced killer be hired to take care of a low-level scrounger like Didi?"

Didi sat erect. "Low-level? Just a minute. I resent that characterization. Haven't you noticed that we painted the windowsills? And as for scrounging —"

"Didi, focus your mind," Qui-Gon interrupted urgently. "Think!"

"Hardly my best ability," Didi said. "But I'll

try. Information has dried up recently. And I've been busy with the café. Astri doesn't like my . . . sideline, so I have to be careful now. However, there are a couple of pieces that came my way recently by way of a regular informant, Fligh. But neither of them seems at all important. I wasn't even sure who to sell them to . . ."

"What are they?" Qui-Gon asked impatiently.

Didi held up one fat finger. "First, Senator Uta S'orn from the planet Belasco is resigning." He held up a second. "And the Tech Raiders are moving their headquarters to Vandor-3."

Obi-Wan looked at Qui-Gon. "Tech Raiders?"

"Black market traders in space vessels and weapons," Qui-Gon explained.

"But why would the gang care if I knew their new location?" Didi asked. "They know I wouldn't sell it to the security forces. I myself have used the gang to find parts for my pocket cruiser." At Qui-Gon's raised eyebrow, he quickly added, "Well, they are cheaper! It's not illegal. Technically."

"Even if the parts are stolen?" Qui-Gon asked.

"I don't know if they're stolen!" Didi insisted. "Why should I ask? I know *I* didn't steal them."

"What about Senator S'orn?" Qui-Gon asked.

Didi shrugged. "She's not on any important committees or planning a war or anything. It's a piece of gossip, nothing more. I'm planning to call on a few journalists. One will probably pay a few credits. I'll have to hurry to beat Fligh. He's been known to sell information more than once. I assure you, this is all routine news. Nothing worth killing anyone over. Especially me."

"We don't know that for sure," Qui-Gon said thoughtfully. "We'll have to investigate both items."

Why us? Obi-Wan thought. They had done one favor for Didi. Did Qui-Gon mean to involve them further?

The door opened and a slender female rushed into the room. She wore a utility cap that was tugged low over her forehead. Curly dark hair poked out of it, waving around her ears and neck. She wore a floor-length apron that was snowy white except for one brilliant splotch of red. As she walked, she left floury footprints. She held a pan full of soup that was the obvious source of the apron stain.

She thrust a spoon at Obi-Wan. "Taste this, will you?"

Obi-Wan glanced at Qui-Gon, mindful of his directive not to eat the food.

"Don't be shy. Here." She pushed the spoon toward him.

Obi-Wan had no choice. Tentatively, he spooned up the soup and swallowed. A smooth, tangy liquid slid down his throat.

"It's good," he said, surprised.

"Really?" Didi and the young woman said together, also surprised.

"Really," Obi-Wan told her.

She turned and saw Qui-Gon. "Qui-Gon! Didi said you were here. How good it is to see you." She placed the pot on the desk, spilling a little over the top. She took the edge of her apron and wiped the spill, knocking a shower of durasheets onto the floor. "Oops."

Didi shot Qui-Gon a warning look that she did not catch.

"Just a friendly visit," Qui-Gon answered. "You're right, Astri. It's been too long since I visited your father."

"Have you seen the improvements?" Astri asked. "I painted everything myself. It was hard to persuade my father to spruce up the place."

"I don't want to scare the regular customers away," Didi said.

"If only we could," Astri groaned.

"I don't know what was wrong with my cooking," Didi went on. "Nobody ever complained."

"Sure," Astri said cheerfully. "They were too busy being sick. Meanwhile, I've decided we must spend money on new napkins, and cloths for the tables —"

"Who needs a cloth? It just gets dirty!"

Astri turned to Qui-Gon and spread her hands. "Do you see my problem? I want to make the place better, and all he does is complain. He welcomes back the dregs of the galaxy. He promised to give up buying and selling information, but he can't resist feeding them. How can I attract a better class of customer when the place is full of gangsters?"

"Everyone likes to eat with gangsters," Didi observed. "It adds spice to the food."

"I'll add the spice, thank you very much," Astri said crisply. "I've landed a big client, Father. This could be our big break. There's a medical conference coming to the Senate, and scientists are arriving from all over the galaxy. Guess who booked the café for a small dinner?"

"The Chancellor?" Didi guessed.

"Not yet," Astri said with a grin. "Jenna Zan Arbor!"

Obi-Wan had heard of Jenna Zan Arbor. Years ago, as a young scientist, she had achieved fame by inventing a vaccine for a world threatened by a deadly space virus. She focused her attention on helping planets with low levels of technology. Her last project was to triple the food supply on the famine-stricken planet of Melasaton.

"Who?" Didi asked.

"Jenna Zan Arbor!" Astri cried. "She reserved the entire café for her party!"

"Did you say elegant?" Didi asked. "Now *that* sounds expensive."

"Just . . . don't . . . ruin it," Astri said through her teeth. Then she picked up the soup and left the room, curls bouncing, apron swinging, and soup dribbling onto the floor.

"Isn't she marvelous?" Didi sighed. "But she is driving me into bankruptcy."

"You promised her not to buy and sell information anymore," Qui-Gon said.

"Well, I suppose I did, yes. But can I help it if this one or that one whispers something to me in exchange for a few credits or a meal?"

"Maybe Didi should go away for awhile," Obi-Wan suggested. "Some other planet where the bounty hunter won't find him."

"Now that's an idea!" Didi said cheerfully. "Running away is just my style!" Then he frowned. "But I don't like to leave Astri."

"Of course not," Qui-Gon agreed.

"She will spend all my money," Didi said.

Qui-Gon sighed. "I don't think you should run away, Didi. The bounty hunter is undoubtedly an expert tracker. And it is better that we face the problem here and now. Obi-Wan and I will do some investigating for you."

"But we're due back at the Temple!" Obi-Wan protested. "Tahl said Yoda was expecting us."

"We can spare a few hours," Qui-Gon said. "I'll contact Yoda on the way and tell him why we are delaying our return. He'll understand. He's a —"

"— friend of Didi's," Obi-Wan supplied.

Qui-Gon's eyes twinkled. "Besides, it will give you a chance to see the seamier side of Coruscant."

"Just what I always wanted," Obi-Wan grumbled.

"And when you return, I'll treat you to a delicious meal!" Didi announced.

Obi-Wan looked doubtful. "As long as you're not the one to cook it," he said.

CHAPTER 5

Armed with a good description of Fligh, the informant, Qui-Gon and Obi-Wan headed to the Senate. "Just ask around," Didi had told them. "Everyone knows Fligh."

They walked through the main entrance of the Senate rotunda. The press of beings inside worked against the calm surroundings to create a sense of controlled chaos. Obi-Wan was jostled and bumped by quick-moving Senatorial aides and consorts of various species. Hover-cams buzzed overhead, heading to the vast interior amphitheater to record the proceedings. Guards dressed in royal blue robes strode by purposefully.

Small cafés were tucked into overhangs along the exterior wall, some more populated than others. Qui-Gon stopped to inquire at several of them, and then moved on.

"Didi is right," he told Obi-Wan. "Everyone knows Fligh. They just don't know where he is."

At last they found him in one of the small pocket cafes. This one was deserted. It was past time for midday meal, and the Senate was in session.

Fligh sat at a small table, nursing a glass of muja juice. He was a spindly creature with a long face, prominent ears, and one green prosthetic eye.

Qui-Gon and Obi-Wan sat at the table. "Didi sent us," Qui-Gon said.

Fligh looked surprised. Then he licked his lips. "Didn't know Jedi trafficked in information. Buy, sell, or trade?"

"We are not here to make a deal," Qui-Gon said. "We need you to tell us how you found out about the two pieces of information you just sold to Didi."

Fligh wrapped his long, thin fingers around his glass and looked at them slyly. "Why should I tell you? What's in it for me, I ask?"

"You would be helping Didi," Qui-Gon said. "He is in trouble. And if you chose not to help him, I would not be pleased." Qui-Gon gave Fligh a level stare.

Fligh choked on his muja juice, then broke out into nervous laughter. "You are a friend of Didi! I am a friend of Didi! We are all friends! There you go! Of course I want you to be pleased. I'll tell you everything you wish to know. May I say that I am both helpful and discreet? And generous. May I offer you two some muja juice? Unfortunately at the moment I am out of credits, but I would be happy to order them for you."

Qui-Gon shook his head. "Just tell us what we want to know, Fligh. How did you find out about the Tech Raiders?"

Fligh shrugged. "Easy. One hears things if one pays attention. And there you go."

"You just heard it in the air?" Qui-Gon asked.

"I can see you're a stickler for details," Fligh said, leaning back and chuckling at Qui-Gon. "Okay, okay. I heard it from their representative on Coruscant. Helb is the broker for stolen tech equipment. One meets him in the Splendor Tavern, he makes the deal. He used to make deals at Didi's, but the lovely Astri took care of that. Too bad — Didi always gave me juice for free." Fligh sighed at the lost opportunity.

"What about your information about Senator S'orn?" Qui-Gon asked.

"One has to protect one's sources, you know," Fligh stalled.

Qui-Gon gave him a stern look. It was all he had to do. The cowardly Fligh immediately backtracked.

"Okay, okay, I can see you'll make me talk. I got hold of a confidential memo written by S'orn herself announcing her resignation. It isn't scheduled to be released until next week. Naturally one could not let such a find go to waste."

"And how did you get this memo?" Qui-Gon asked.

"How does one learn things? Things happen. A durasheet falls into the trash bin, someone plucks it out, passes it along . . ." Fligh shrugged. "It's the way one has to work. A little here, a little there. A favor here, a trade there, and there you go." He turned to Obi-Wan. "Do you like my eye?"

The abrupt question took Obi-Wan by surprise. "Which one?" he asked politely.

"The green one, of course!" Fligh said, pointing to it. "I lost my own in a little dustup with some Hutts. Isn't it a beauty?"

"It's very attractive," Obi-Wan said.

"Very nice," Qui-Gon offered, when Fligh turned to him.

"You see? There you go — a trade. A little information goes here, a little goes there, and I get an eye! How else does one survive on Coruscant?"

"One could get a job," Qui-Gon pointed out.

"One could, if one were a different being," Fligh agreed. "However, one is not." He shrugged again. "I do the best I can. On my own since I was knee-high, I learned how to get by. Didi is my friend. He has done much for me, and Astri is in my heart as well. I'm sorry Didi is in trouble. I will try to help, Jedi. This I promise."

"I think it better if you stay out of it," Qui-Gon said in a kindly tone, for Fligh's tone was sincere. "We don't know what we're dealing with yet."

"Then call on me when you need me. I will do my best, which I am sure you can guess is not much." Fligh cackled. "But there you go."

Qui-Gon stood. "We might have to return and ask you more questions."

"I am always here," Fligh said. He waved at the empty café and his jar of muja juice. "Where else can one find such excitement?"

Since they were already in the Senate building, Qui-Gon decided that their next stop should be Senator Uta S'orn's office.

The outer room was empty, so Qui-Gon knocked on an inner door.

"Telissa?" The door was flung open. A Belascan female stood, one hand on her hip, wearing the trademark Belascan headdress of wrapped jeweled cloth, as well as an irritable expression. "Oh, sorry. I thought you were my assistant." Her glittering eyes swept them, and her expression changed. "Oh. Jedi. Excuse my rudeness."

"May we speak with you for a moment?" Qui-Gon asked.

"I am very busy . . . all right. Enter." Senator S'orn swiveled and walked back into her private office. She waved them to two chairs set in front of her desk.

Qui-Gon seated himself and began with preliminaries. "You are resigning next week, Senator S'orn."

She looked startled. "But how do you know this?"

"The information is out there," Qui-Gon said. "It is for sale. I do not know if anyone has bought it yet, but no doubt someone will. We cannot prevent that."

Senator S'orn dropped her head in her hands. "My data pad. It was stolen at the Senate commissary. My resignation announcement was on it."

Obi-Wan glanced at Qui-Gon. Obviously, Fligh had lied about how he'd received the information.

She raised her head. "Disaster. I'm sponsoring legislation in two days. If this gets out beforehand, I'll have no support."

"Did you see anyone nearby who could have stolen it?" Qui-Gon asked.

She shook her head. "Just the usual Senate crowd." She laced her fingers together and bowed her head for a moment in thought. Then she raised her head and put both hands flat on the desk. "Decision. I must announce my resignation immediately. Then I can rally supporters to the legislation by saying they must help me with my legacy. I'll play on their sympathies." She drummed her fingers on the desk as she calculated her strategy. Her mind seemed to be elsewhere as she said absently, "Thank you for telling me."

Qui-Gon stood. "Thank you for your time."

She did not say good-bye or acknowledge them again. Her mind was already working to fix her problem. Obi-Wan followed Qui-Gon out the door.

"Why didn't you ask her about Didi?" he asked Qui-Gon.

"Because it wouldn't have gotten me anywhere. If she put a death mark on Didi's head, she would hardly admit it," Qui-Gon said. "And I can't see how she could trace the theft of the data pad to Didi. Do you?"

"Only if she's lying," Obi-Wan said after a moment. "If she'd seen Fligh steal it, it would be easy to trace him to Didi. But why go after Didi, and not Fligh?"

Obi-Wan thought this over some more. He

felt at a disadvantage. Qui-Gon seemed to have an insight into the hearts and minds of beings that he did not.

"Still, Senator S'orn's distress seemed sincere to me," he said slowly. "She was barely polite and not terribly nice, but not evil. Just busy."

"A typical Senator," Qui-Gon said with a half smile.

"She seemed surprised that the information was out," Obi-Wan said.

"Yes, she did," Qui-Gon mused. "Unless she is a very good actress. But she did seem sincerely upset."

"Why did Fligh tell us that an assistant got her announcement out of the trash?" Obi-Wan asked. "It's obviously not true."

"He didn't actually say that, Padawan," Qui-Gon said. "He just indicated that as one of many ways he could have gotten the information. No, Fligh stole the data pad. He would not want to admit that to us, however."

"This seems like a dead end to me," Obi-Wan said in conclusion. "Senator S'orn certainly doesn't look like a murderer."

Qui-Gon's blue eyes were keen. "Tell me, Padawan. What does a murderer look like?"

CHAPTER 6

The wide Senate doors at the south exit were crowded with beings hurrying inside and outside the building. They were all intent on getting somewhere fast, some of them barking into comlinks, others with harried, preoccupied looks on their faces.

"Now we need to find the Splendor Tavern," Obi-Wan said.

"I know where it is," Qui-Gon answered, striking off to his left down a small alley.

Obi-Wan lengthened his stride to match his Master's. "How do you know?" he asked curiously.

"Because I have had occasion to go there," Qui-Gon responded. "It's where connections are made for the black market. If one needs weapons or an illegally modified speeder, or wants to gamble, one goes to the Splendor.

Sometimes on a mission you need help from the worst sorts as well as the best."

Qui-Gon led him farther into a section he had never been in before, down many levels closer to the planet's surface. If Obi-Wan had been asked to describe Coruscant, he would have talked of a gleaming planet, all silver and white, with wide walkways and space lanes that flashed with agile crafts zooming toward their destinations. He barely knew the other Coruscant, below the levels of the Senate and the beautiful residences above. This one was made up of narrow alleys and cluttered streets, with dark shadows and furtive creatures who darted away when they saw the Jedi striding toward them. Games of chance were played on stoops and in outdoor cafés. Weapons were placed on tables as warnings for cheaters.

Qui-Gon stopped in front of a metal building with a sagging roof. An old readout sign swung in front, occasionally banging against the rough metal walls with a screeching sound. Half of its letters had burned out, so it read: S P   D O R. The windows were shuttered, and only a thin strip of light came through.

"Here we are," Qui-Gon said.

"Here?" Obi-Wan studied the building with a dubious eye. "It certainly doesn't live up to its name."

"Don't worry. It's worse than it looks."

Qui-Gon pushed open the door. Immediately they were met with a blast of noise. Music played from a recorder in the corner while a variety of customers drank, ate, and played games of chance at each table. A jubilee wheel whirled on the bar, and gamblers gathered around with fistfuls of credits, betting on the outcome. It stopped, and one crowed triumphantly while two others began to fight. A fourth turned away, desperation on his face.

Qui-Gon made his way to the Imbat bartender, whose head nearly bumped the ceiling, and whose long ears drooped to his shoulders. As the Jedi watched, his massive hand reached out and casually smacked a bar customer who was trying to get his attention by waving his arms. The customer fell back off his seat and crashed to the floor, a stunned look on his face. Someone stepped over him and took his place.

With a jolt, Obi-Wan realized that Didi's café hadn't been filled with the worst of the galaxy, as he'd thought. He did not know who owned the Splendor. But whoever it was obviously did not care one bit about his customers.

Qui-Gon took up a position at the end of the bar. He did not signal the bartender in any way, but the Imbat moved toward him. He bent his massive head and listened to Qui-Gon dolefully.

Then, moving only his eyes, he indicated a shadowy corner.

Qui-Gon signaled to Obi-Wan, and they moved toward it.

Helb was a Neimoidian. Instead of the large glasses of ale the other customers were swilling, a small cup of tea was almost hidden in his large, sharp-nailed hands. Though Neimoidians usually favored the richest robes they could afford, Helb wore a plain gray unisuit with two blasters strapped to his hips. His back was to the wall, and he watched the crowd with shrewd orange eyes.

Qui-Gon took a seat at the table across from him. Obi-Wan did the same.

Helb gave them a considering look. "I am surprised to see Jedi in a place such as this."

"We come for information only," Qui-Gon said.

"That is probably the one thing I do not have to sell," Helb said.

"That is all right, for I do not wish to buy it," Qui-Gon said. He sat in silence, waiting. Again, Obi-Wan marveled at how much Qui-Gon was able to convey through stillness.

Helb gave the hissing sound that passed for Neimoidian laughter. "You are lucky. I'm in a good mood. I just won a game of sabacc. Otherwise you would be talking to a wall."

Qui-Gon didn't rise to the bait. "There is a death mark on the head of Didi Oddo. He wonders if the Tech Raiders are displeased with him."

Helb laughed again. "*I* am the one who is displeased with Didi. He beat me at a game of sabacc the other day. That is why I am so happy to win today."

Qui-Gon nodded. Helb took a sip of tea.

"Which doesn't mean I want to kill him," Helb continued. "If I were going to put a death mark on someone's head, it would be his friend Fligh."

"Why?" Qui-Gon asked.

"Because he owes the Tech Raiders an interesting sum of money," Helb responded. "Not just gambling winnings on one game of sabacc, but favor after favor we have done him for which he has not paid. Why would I put a contract out on Didi?"

"Because if you put a death mark on Fligh, you'd never get your money," Qui-Gon said.

Helb laughed. "I'll never get it anyway!"

"Fligh knows that your group has moved to Vandor-3," Qui-Gon said. "If you kill him, the information won't get out."

Helb shook his head, bemused. "I told Fligh because I *wanted* the information to get out. I knew he wouldn't sell it to the security force.

Only to those who need tech equipment or stolen speeders for cheap. How else would we get customers? Speaking of which, if the Temple needs equipment . . ."

"No, thank you," Qui-Gon said. He stood.

"Don't worry about Didi," Helb said. "He always seems to land on his feet. And if you see Fligh, tell him I'm looking for him. That should scare him!" Hissing with amusement, Helb turned his attention back to his tea.

Qui-Gon started for the door. As Obi-Wan began to follow, something caught his eye. A wizened old man wrapped in layers of soiled cloaks and robes sat at a table, pushing pieces around a gameboard with a dirty finger. His eyes slowly slid back to the board as Obi-Wan glanced at him. A jolt of familiarity hit Obi-Wan, but he could not place it.

He caught up with Qui-Gon at the door. But something made him turn back. The old man was now heading toward the back of the place. He shuffled through the crowd at first, but his step quickened as he passed through the throng at the bar. It was difficult to keep him in sight through the press of bodies, but Obi-Wan focused his attention, watching for movement.

He saw a cape drop to the floor. Then another. No one noticed.

The windows along the back were shuttered as well. One was slightly more ajar than the others, the window itself cracked to let in a tiny stream of air.

The shuffling old man had disappeared. A tall female dressed in a dark tunic suddenly disengaged from the crowd and moved toward the rear.

"It's her," Obi-Wan breathed. He quickly turned to Qui-Gon. "She's here."

Qui-Gon turned. As they watched, the female dressed in black hauled herself up and then slipped through the narrow opening of the window, her body seeming to compress as she did so.

With a leap, Qui-Gon burst out the front door. Obi-Wan followed on his heels. They raced down a narrow alleyway crowded with so many durasteel garbage bins that they had to leap up and run on top of them.

Garbage squished under their boots, impeding their progress. They landed as lightly as they could, racing over the tops of the bins toward the rear. At the end of the alleyway, they leaped down onto solid ground.

She was already disappearing around a corner far down the back alley.

Qui-Gon increased his pace, and Obi-Wan

spurted forward to catch up to him. His Master was a faster runner, and he dashed around the corner before Obi-Wan could get there.

Obi-Wan pushed himself to his limit, racing after Qui-Gon. The question was, if they caught the bounty hunter, what would they do? Questioning her had not exactly been productive before.

As he rounded the corner, he saw that Qui-Gon had given up. The alley widened into a small square with six different roads radiating out from the center.

"She's gone," Qui-Gon said.

"If that was really her," Obi-Wan said. "Now I can't quite believe it. I saw an old man, and suddenly he became a younger female."

"Your eyes did not deceive you, Obi-Wan," Qui-Gon said. "Only a Sorussian would have been able to slip through that opening. The question is, why was she there at all? Was it a coincidence, or is she now on our trail?"

CHAPTER 7

"What are you doing here?" Astri demanded as Qui-Gon and Obi-Wan walked through the door of Didi's Café. She wiped her flour-dusted hands on a dish towel. "Oh, forgive me, I didn't mean that the way it sounded. You are always welcome, Qui-Gon. Except not just now."

"Don't worry, Astri, we haven't come for a meal," Qui-Gon told her.

"Jenna Zan Arbor is due with her party any moment," Astri said distractedly. "One of the servers hasn't shown up. I haven't finished the banja cakes yet. The water won't boil for the pashi noodles, and my sauce is too spicy!"

"It smells delicious," Obi-Wan said helpfully.

"Thank you. If only I could feed them with smells! How does the place look? Fligh was supposed to come by and sweep, and he never showed up, that rascal. After all Didi has done for him!"

"I have never seen the café look better," Qui-Gon assured her.

Astri had tried to brighten the place with ornate candles on the two long tables she had pushed together. A long pink cloth was on each table, and the plates and glasses looked clean and sparkling. But she could not hide the general air of disrepair of the place. The walls were dingy with the years of smoke and dirt, and the floor was pitted from the marks of thousands of boots and scuffles.

"There was no time to paint the inside," Astri said, noticing Obi-Wan's glance around. "And no time to tear the place down and rebuild, either." She gave a comical grimace.

"I'm sure everything will go fine," Qui-Gon said. "We've just come to talk to Didi for a moment. Is he here?"

"He's in the back. I told him to stay out of my way." Astri's dark eyes twinkled. "I think I scared him. He actually listened to me." Suddenly, she craned her neck and stared out the window. "Stars and planets, it's them!" Astri gave a surprisingly loud bellow. "Renzii! Our customers are here! Renzii —"

She was still bellowing as the door opened.

A tall woman dressed in a gray shimmersilk gown underneath a rich purple cloak stood uncertainly in the doorway. Her gleaming blond hair was intertwined with silky fabric. "This is Didi's Café?"

Hurriedly, Astri wiped her hands on her stained apron, then held one out for the woman to shake. She had rubbed a berry stain on her apron, and the hand she offered was blue. The woman stared at it and did not take it. Astri quickly tucked her hand behind her back.

"Yes, yes, come in. You are so welcome. I'm the owner and chef, Astri Oddo."

Qui-Gon and Obi-Wan faded back. The woman's party crowded behind her. They glanced around the café, surprise on their faces. Obviously they had expected a grander restaurant for their meal. They were from various worlds, but all had a prosperous look. The men were dressed in fine tunics and jackets, the women in shimmersilk gowns or jackets. One aristocratic-looking female wore a jeweled turban. Her light blue eyes widened in dismay as she surveyed the café, and she quickly gathered her tunic closer around her.

"There must be some mistake," Jenna Zan Arbor said.

Just then Renzii the waiter raced out of the kitchen and skidded to a stop in front of the party, still buttoning his tunic. "Welcome, come in, enter, this way," he babbled.

"I think we'd better leave Astri to her guests,"

Qui-Gon murmured to Obi-Wan. "It seems her hands are full."

They walked back toward Didi's private office. They pushed open the door. Didi sat in a chair, his back to them. He didn't turn.

"Didi? Is everything all right?" Qui-Gon asked.

Slowly, the chair swiveled around to face them. Didi's dark eyes were full of tears. "I fear it is my fault," he said.

"What is your fault, Didi?" Qui-Gon asked gently.

"It's Fligh," he said. "He's been murdered."

CHAPTER 8

Obi-Wan had faced death before. He never
got used to it. The way a spirit could fill a space,
the life energy behind the eyes, and then . . .
nothing.

"What happened?" Qui-Gon demanded.

"I don't know," Didi said, mopping his face
with a napkin. "The Coruscant security force
contacted me. They know Fligh is a friend. He
was found in one of the alleyways around the
Senate. The Lane of All Worlds is where he is lying like an animal." Perspiration shone on Didi's
face. "Do you think this has anything to do with
me?" he asked. His face betrayed how fearful
he was to hear the answer.

"I'm afraid I do," Qui-Gon said grimly. "We'd
better talk to the security forces. Come on,
Didi."

"Me?" Didi squeaked. "Why do I have to go?"

"Because I think you should remain with us at

all times now," Qui-Gon said. "You aren't safe here."

"But I am!" Didi protested. "Astri will lock the front door so no other customers come. And this fancy party will go on for hours. No one will try to attack me while such distinguished guests are here. And besides," he added in a low tone, "I'm too afraid and sad to move right now. I could not look upon my dead friend's body. I am sorry."

Qui-Gon exchanged a glance with Obi-Wan. Obi-Wan hoped he was not going to suggest that he stay here with Didi while Qui-Gon investigated Fligh's death. He did not want to stay behind to baby-sit Didi when there was work to do.

"All right," Qui-Gon said reluctantly. "This shouldn't take very long. Make sure every door and window is fastened tight, Didi. This bounty hunter can get through very small spaces."

Didi nodded vigorously. "I have done so already, but I will double-check."

"We'll return soon," Qui-Gon said. "We'll knock at the back door. I don't want to spoil Astri's big evening."

"So considerate of you, Qui-Gon," Didi said fervently. "None of us want to spoil things for Astri. I will wait here. Can you . . . can you make sure that Fligh is . . . taken care of?" Didi's eyes filled with tears. "Tell the security forces that I will pay for the funeral. I will pay for everything."

Qui-Gon put a hand on Didi's shoulder. "This is not your fault, my friend."

"I hear your words," Didi whispered. "Yet I do not feel them."

Qui-Gon checked the doors and windows from the outside before they headed off. He did not trust the scattered Astri to remember to bolt the door. But everything was locked up tight.

It was fully dark when Qui-Gon and Obi-Wan arrived at the Lane of All Worlds. There was no moon, and the glare of the glow lamps threw harsh shadows.

The Coruscant security forces in their navy uniforms milled around Fligh's fallen body, which was covered by a tarp.

"May I look?" Qui-Gon asked the officer in charge. His nameplate read CAPTAIN YUR T'AUG. He was a stocky Bothan with a flowing beard and glossy dark hair that hung to his shoulders.

The captain frowned, but all officers in the security force knew that Jedi requests must be honored.

"All right," Captain Yur T'aug said. "Not a pleasant sight, though."

"Stay here, Padawan," Qui-Gon told Obi-Wan. This order Obi-Wan was glad to obey. He did not want to see Fligh's body. He wanted to remember Fligh alive.

He watched as Qui-Gon, his back to him, crouched to lift a corner of the tarp. Although Qui-Gon did not flinch or shudder, Obi-Wan knew the sight had distressed him. There was something about how his Master did not move for several seconds, how his hand dropped the tarp with great gentleness.

Obi-Wan turned away with a shudder. Around the body, officers went about the business of death, tagging various items, searching the ground with glow rods, entering information in their data pads, talking in groups. It could be any being lying on that cold stone walkway. Fligh had ceased to matter. Only the manner of his death was important.

Obi-Wan looked up at the dark sky. Stars glittered with edges that looked hard enough to cut. Already he felt at times that he had seen too much death and cruelty. How did Qui-Gon, who had seen so much more, feel? It was the Jedi's job to meet such things. To help. The helping was easy compared to this.

Will I ever get used to death? Obi-Wan wondered.

Obi-Wan saw something glitter in the dim shadows. He walked closer. It was a bright green stone. He leaned down to study it and realized it was Fligh's prosthetic eye. It must have rolled away from the body. He pointed it out to Qui-Gon, who nodded.

Qui-Gon showed it to Captain Yur T'aug. "It belonged to the victim," he said.

The captain crouched to examine it. "Sergeant!" he called. "Tag this item."

Another officer scurried over with a specimen bag and carefully picked up the eye with a tweezer device.

"What was the cause of death?" Qui-Gon asked quietly.

"Strangulation, we believe," Captain Yur T'aug said shortly.

"I saw the marks," Qui-Gon said. "It seems like a slender cord of some kind. Not hands."

The captain nodded.

"And the unusual . . . ah, pallor?" Qui-Gon asked.

"The body was drained of blood," Captain Yur T'aug said. "He was killed elsewhere and then dropped off here."

Obi-Wan looked back at the tarp and shuddered again.

Qui-Gon's voice was calm. "Any suspects?"

The captain sighed, tapping his comlink with an impatient finger. "I should be investigating, not filling you in. You can read the report when I am done."

Qui-Gon did not show his impatience, but Obi-Wan could feel it. "I do not have time to read your report," he said, his voice as brittle as ice.

Captain Yur T'aug hesitated, then said, "No suspects yet. Nobody saw anything. But we know this Fligh character. He's a well-known informant and petty thief. Could have a hundred enemies. Not to mention that he owes money all over town. I hear he has a major debt to the Tech Raiders."

Qui-Gon studied the officer for a moment. "There is something else," he said.

"This is not the first body we've found drained of blood," Captain Yur T'aug said hesitantly. "Drifters, lowlifes — beings no one would miss. Over the past year, there have been a half dozen. Maybe more we haven't found. Who knows? Coruscant can be a hard world. Many transients come here to scrounge a living."

"If this is the case, the killer is most likely not someone Fligh owed money to," Qui-Gon said.

Captain Yur T'aug shrugged. "Or else the killer copied the method to throw us off the track. It's our job to find out."

"You might want to check into a female bounty hunter," Qui-Gon said. "She's a Sorussian who might have had reason to dispose of

Fligh. She's been staying at the Soft Landings Inn."

"Sure," Captain Yur T'aug said. "Thanks for the tip." His lack of interest was obvious.

"Good luck to you," Qui-Gon said. "You should know that Didi Oddo will pay for the funeral. Fligh was not friendless. He will be missed."

Qui-Gon motioned to Obi-Wan, and they walked past the officers back onto the main walkway that curved around the Senate.

"Are you all right, Padawan?" Qui-Gon asked him.

"Fligh wasn't my friend," Obi-Wan said. "I only spent a few minutes with him. There was something likeable about him, but I can't say that I liked him. Yet I feel almost as sad as Didi."

"I do as well," Qui-Gon said.

They walked a few steps in silence. "Do you ever get used to death?" Obi-Wan asked.

"No," Qui-Gon said. "That is how it should be."

"Why do you think Fligh was killed?" Obi-Wan asked. "Do you think that he knew something important but didn't realize it, like Didi?"

"Perhaps," Qui-Gon said. "And remember that Fligh said he would try to help Didi. I wonder if he *did* try. No doubt it would be easy for him to discover where the bounty hunter was lodging."

"You think that is what happened?" Obi-Wan asked.

"Let us swing by the inn on the way back to the café," Qui-Gon suggested. "We should have another talk with this bounty hunter."

They walked quickly through the streets until they reached the Soft Landings Inn. This time the front door was slightly ajar, so they were able to walk in without ringing the innkeeper. They quickly climbed the stairs to the third level. Qui-Gon knocked on the door, and it swung open. The room was empty.

"She's gone." The Togorian stood behind them with a bucket and vibro-mop. "Checked out. I have to clean. Get out of my way."

They retreated down the stairs. "I don't like this," Qui-Gon murmured. "Let's get back to Didi's."

They quickened their pace and began to run. Didi's wasn't far.

They swung around the corner. Ahead was the café. There was no spill of light from the windows, and the front door was shut tight.

"We are too late," Qui-Gon said.

CHAPTER 9

Lightsabers drawn, they rushed into the café. With a quick sweep, they saw that it was empty. Plates with half-eaten food sat on the tables. Qui-Gon charged past the tables to the kitchen. Pots were overturned, their contents on the floor. Bins of flour and grain spilled onto the counters. The cooler door was open.

They ran to Didi's private office. Papers and files were thrown on the floor, the contents of durasteel bins upended and kicked through. Everything on the shelves had been tossed onto the floor.

"Upstairs," Qui-Gon barked.

He raced up, Obi-Wan on his heels. They burst into Didi's private quarters together.

In times of danger, Qui-Gon's senses slowed down. He took in everything in the room in what felt like several long seconds but was more likely the flicker of an eyelash. Astri on the floor, unconscious or dead. Didi standing, wrapped in the bounty hunter's whip, his eyes wide with terror, a bruise on his forehead. And the bounty hunter turning, pausing for an instant when she saw them. Her expressionless gaze showed no surprise, no fear.

Real time snapped back. Qui-Gon anticipated the bounty hunter's reach to the blaster strapped to her thigh. He moved forward to counterattack. He did not anticipate that she would aim at Astri, not at him. His Jedi reflexes were fast enough so that he was able to spin and turn, sweeping his lightsaber wide. He was slightly off-balance, but he managed to deflect the fire.

Astri stirred. Relief streamed through him. She was alive.

A perfect attack blended deception with speed and strategy. Qui-Gon feinted a pass to the bounty hunter's left and instead charged straight at her. She did not respond to the feint but fired straight, then leaped high to the left to avoid him. His lightsaber whizzed through empty air where she'd been.

She was even better than he'd thought.

Obi-Wan moved forward to cover Astri so that Qui-Gon could concentrate on the attack. The bounty hunter activated her whip and retracted it. It spun off Didi in a dizzying circle, sending him flying against the wall. He hit it with a thud and fell to the floor, dazed.

The whip reverted to laser mode. With a slashing maneuver, the bounty hunter shattered the transparisteel in the window. Qui-Gon sprang forward, still keeping his body between his opponent and Astri. Didi began to crawl toward his daughter, getting underneath Qui-Gon's feet. Qui-Gon jumped to avoid him, his attention now focused on protecting Didi.

The bounty hunter leaped out the window. Outside was a small enclosure that held various speeders and swoops. She jumped into one and took off.

Qui-Gon stood at the window as the lights of the swoop twinkled and receded. He felt anger rock him, and he took a minute to accept and release it. His opponent had eluded him. Sometimes it happened. He had fought the best fight he could.

But she has eluded me three times now.

"Astri," Didi said brokenly. "Astri . . ."

Qui-Gon knelt by the young woman's side. He felt carefully around her skull. "What happened?" he asked Didi. "Did she get hit by blaster fire?"

"No, no. Knocked out from behind," Didi said. "With the handle of the whip."

Qui-Gon felt a lump rising on Astri's skull. Her

eyes fluttered open. Her pupils were not dilated and her eyes focused on his face.

"Ouch," she said.

"She's all right," he said to Didi. "Lie still, Astri. You're going to have a headache."

She let out a hiss of air. "I'll say."

"We should call a medic," Didi said worriedly.

"I'm all right," Astri said. Wincing, she raised herself on her elbows. "What happened? The last thing I remember is all my customers going out the door."

"Did anyone come in while they were going out?" Qui-Gon asked.

"No," Astri said. "I locked the door behind them and told Renzii to go home. Locked the door behind him, too. Then I came upstairs. That's all I remember . . ."

"I was up here," Didi said. "I heard Astri on the stairs. She opened the door and suddenly fell down. Then the bounty hunter came in. She tied me up while she searched the place. She went downstairs and I heard her searching my private office."

"And the kitchen," Qui-Gon said.

"No, not the kitchen," Didi said.

"But it was chaos, pots everywhere," Obi-Wan said.

"It always looks that way," Astri said with a

sigh. "What bounty hunter? I thought we were talking about a common thief."

"Why did the group leave?" Qui-Gon asked Astri.

Astri cradled her head in her hands. "I tried my best," she mumbled. "I guess I'm not quite elegant yet. Renzii kept mixing up the orders. I couldn't handle all the cooking. Some of the food was cold. So Jenna Zan Arbor had a fit, and they left. Next time I'll hire extra help. That was a big mistake. It's just that I spent all the extra money on the food . . ."

"So how did the bounty hunter get in?" Obi-Wan asked.

Astri lifted her head. "*What bounty hunter?*" she asked again in frustration.

"Didi, tell her," Qui-Gon said.

"Not while you're hurt, Astri," Didi said nervously. "You need to lie down —"

"*What* bounty hunter?" Astri asked through clenched teeth.

"I might—ah—have gotten myself in a tiny spot of trouble," Didi told her. "Nothing serious."

"Sure," Astri said. "This isn't serious. Just another ordinary evening in the café. I get knocked out on a regular basis."

"What a sense of humor my daughter has,"

Didi said to the Jedi nervously. "Isn't she marvelous?"

"Your father may have a piece of information that is valuable to someone," Qui-Gon broke in impatiently. "That someone has sent a bounty hunter after him. We're assuming they want the information back at any cost. And yet, the bounty hunter did not kill him when she had the chance."

"That's a good sign," Didi said encouragingly. Then he looked fearful again. "Isn't it?"

"You're selling information again?" Astri yelled angrily. Then she winced and closed her eyes. She lowered her voice to a whisper. "You slimy, slithery, snaky son of a Kowakian monkey-lizard," she hissed through her teeth. "You lied to me. Again."

"I didn't lie so much as not tell you everything," Didi said, patting her shoulder. "I would not say that I have the thriving business I once did. But Fligh still came to me with bits and pieces to sell. How could I abandon him? Without me, how could he sell his little tidbits? It is tragic that he has been killed."

"Killed? See where his *business* has gotten him," Astri said, fixing her father with a steady stare. "Am I next, Papa?"

Didi turned away, unable to face his daughter. She got up unsteadily and left the room.

"Let's return to what we know," Qui-Gon said

to Didi. "The bounty hunter has not found what she is looking for. She tore this place apart. That means there is an actual object she wants, not just information in your head. What is it, Didi? This time you must tell the complete truth. You see now that you have put the ones you love in danger."

"Yes," Didi said heavily. "I see that. But I cannot help you, my friend. I do not have anything. Fligh didn't give me anything but information. This I swear."

"Not a data pad?" Qui-Gon asked.

Didi shook his head. "Nothing."

Qui-Gon sighed. "Then there is no alternative. You must close up the café. Take Astri and leave Coruscant."

Astri was just returning to the room as Qui-Gon finished. She paused in the act of pressing a cold cloth to her head. "Close up the café?"

"Just until we know what the bounty hunter is looking for," Qui-Gon told her. "We can't stay by your side all day and all night, Astri. I think you are in danger as well as Didi." He paused, then said gently, "I know you are angry at your father, but you do not want to see him hurt."

Astri bit her lip and nodded. "But where will we go?"

"I know where," Didi said. "I have a house in the Cascardi Mountains."

"You bought a *house*?" Astri exclaimed. "But you say you have no money!"

"It was a deal I could not refuse," Didi explained. "I haven't even been there yet, and I haven't told anyone about it."

"Where are the Cascardi Mountains?" Obi-Wan asked.

"On the planet Duneeden," Qui-Gon said. "A short journey from Coruscant. But the mountains are a good choice. The Cascardis are remote and rugged. It's a good hideout for a time. Obi-Wan and I will wait while you pack a few things. You must leave quickly."

Didi sprang up and helped Astri from the room. They went into their bedrooms to pack.

"Do you think they'll be safe?" Obi-Wan asked Qui-Gon in a low tone.

"Safer than here on Coruscant," Qui-Gon said. "But the bounty hunter is no doubt an expert tracker. Even though the galaxy is wide, it's hard for beings to just disappear. No, I fear we must unravel this mystery. No matter where they are, Didi and Astri are still in great danger. She will find them, and it will be sooner rather than later. Of that I have no doubt."

CHAPTER 10

As they entered the cool halls of the Jedi Temple, Qui-Gon saw the relief Obi-Wan tried to hide. The boy was worn out. Qui-Gon had not expected that a short stop to meet Didi would spiral into a twisting mystery they would be forced to solve.

"I did not plan for this, Padawan," he told him. "I just wanted to stop by to say hello to a friend."

Obi-Wan nodded. "But a friend was in danger. You could not refuse to help."

"You did not approve," Qui-Gon said.

He saw the hesitation on Obi-Wan's face. He knew the look well. Obi-Wan hated to disappoint him. But he never lied to him.

"No," he said. "Not at first. But now I do. You say I need to connect to the living Force. More and more I see what you mean. My first impulse was to turn away from Didi." Obi-Wan met his

Master's eyes. "I was tired and hungry and I did not like Didi. I thought of my own needs. Now I see what you see. Didi has faults, but he is a good being. It just takes me longer to see these things. I wish," Obi-Wan said with difficulty, "it did not."

"You are too hard on yourself, Padawan," Qui-Gon said quietly. "That can become a fault if you are not careful, for anger at oneself is a destructive thing. Every living being can be impatient, can turn away at a first glance, can avoid getting involved. It is a natural impulse. We are all creatures who want peace and comfort. Yet we are Jedi. Our own peace and comfort is not what drives us. We are dedicated to a larger good. But always remember that the peace and comfort of just one being is what drives us, too."

Obi-Wan nodded. Qui-Gon put a gentle hand on his shoulder.

"Get something to eat, Padawan," he said. "I am going to speak with Yoda and Tahl."

Qui-Gon could see Obi-Wan's hunger and fatigue battle with his desire to remain by his Master's side. "Are you certain you won't need me?"

"I will find you when I need you," Qui-Gon said. "What you need is a bit of rest and food. Then we'll continue."

He left Obi-Wan at the juncture toward the

food hall. Then he made his way to the Room of a Thousand Fountains, where he was to meet Yoda and Tahl. He had contacted them on his comlink to arrange the meeting.

The cool, moist air revived Qui-Gon better than a meal would have. His eyes rested on the multitude of shades of green in the plants and trees that were arranged amid the winding paths. He paused for a moment to register the beauty around him. He drew a long breath, then another, concentrating on the shades of green, the murmuring fountains, the scent of growth and flowers. He let the moment matter, fill his heart and mind. Refreshed, he headed down the winding paths toward Yoda and Tahl.

They sat on a bench that Yoda favored, where water ran over smooth white pebbles, making a musical sound. Tahl must have heard his step, for she turned her head toward him.

"I hope you allowed Obi-Wan to get a decent meal," she called in a humorous tone before he could speak. "That poor boy is always hungry."

Qui-Gon grinned. Tahl never said hello. Instead she always launched right into a conversation. "Do you realize," he said, seating himself on a bench opposite them, "that you always give me an accusation, never a greeting?"

Tahl smiled. "Of course. How else can I keep you on your toes?"

Qui-Gon let his eyes rest on Tahl's lovely face. Her sightless green-and-gold striped eyes were alive with humor. Once he had not been able to look upon her without pain. Just the sight of the white scar that marked her dark honey skin had grieved him. But he had come to realize how Tahl had accepted her fate, how she had allowed it to deepen her. Her friendship was invaluable to him.

"I left him at the food hall," Qui-Gon said. "I am sure he's on his second helping by now."

"No news have you?" Yoda asked. "Concerned we are about Didi. A scoundrel he may be, but a friend to the Temple he is."

"I am sorry to report that things are worse rather than better," Qui-Gon said. Quickly, he filled them in on the murder of Fligh and the attack on Astri and Didi.

"Fligh's body was drained of blood?" Tahl frowned. "That sounds familiar."

"There have been a half dozen similar cases on Coruscant over the past year," Qui-Gon said. "Mostly drifters, beings with no ties to anyone."

"Yes, I know that," Tahl said. "It is something else." Her frown deepened. "There is one more thing. I did some more investigating on your bounty hunter. It seems she is a master of disguise. She uses wigs, synth-flesh, prosthetics . . . that is how she moves about undetected."

"I am not surprised to hear it," Qui-Gon said. "Obi-Wan saw her turn from an elderly man back into a young woman."

"Say you did that Fligh stole a data pad from a Senator," Yoda said. "Who?"

"Someone I did not know," Qui-Gon said. "Senator Uta S'orn from the planet Belasco."

"By the way, I contacted the security police," Tahl told him. "Senator S'orn never reported the theft. It might not be significant. The Senate is full of petty thieves. I'm sure many thefts do not get reported. Still, I thought I'd mention it. Senator S'orn also announced her resignation today. She said it was for personal reasons."

"Know Senator S'orn, I do," Yoda said. "Several talks she had with the Jedi."

Startled, Qui-Gon turned to Yoda. "About what?"

"A son she had," Yoda continued. "Ren S'orn. Force-sensitive, he was. Accepted him for training, we did. Part with him, his mother could not. Harness the Force, understand it, he could not. Wandered he did through the galaxy."

Tahl gave a sharp intake of breath. "Of course," she whispered. Yoda nodded.

"What is it?" Qui-Gon asked, leaning forward urgently. He saw that Yoda and Tahl knew something important.

"Ren became a lost being, a drifter," Tahl said. "He lost contact with his mother. At last she came to us for help. Several teams of Jedi were sent to find him and help him. He rejected them."

"Hoped we did that he would reach out one day," Yoda said. "Feared we did that he would use the Force for evil. Yet the Force merely confused and angered him. Different he was. Different he did not want to be. Peace he could not find."

"Such a tragedy," Tahl said. "He could not find a way to flourish. He could not find a place that felt like home. So as it often happens he fell in with bad companions. We received word that he had been killed."

"Not long ago, it was," Yoda said. "Six months, I think. On Simpla-12."

"This is sad news," Qui-Gon said. "But why is it significant?"

"Because of the manner of his death," Tahl said quietly. "Ren had been strangled. And his body had been drained of blood."

CHAPTER 11

Obi-Wan saw at once from Qui-Gon's grim face that he would not get to savor his tart. He scrambled to his feet.

"I am sorry, Padawan. But it is time to go," Qui-Gon said.

Obi-Wan snatched up the tart and wolfed it down while they walked. Qui-Gon checked out a speeder from the transport pool. Within seconds, they were heading back toward the Senate building.

It was late evening, and the air lanes still buzzed with traffic. The glow lights made the buildings and walkways blaze as bright as daylight. Beings strolled below them, crowding the restaurants and walkways.

"What did Yoda and Tahl say?" Obi-Wan asked, swallowing the last bite of his tart.

"I don't have a clear picture yet," Qui-Gon told him. "But somehow Senator S'orn is either connected to Fligh's death or involved in it. Her son died the same way Fligh did." Qui-Gon explained the story of Ren's confused life and tragic death.

"But what does that have to do with Didi?" Obi-Wan asked.

"Maybe nothing." Qui-Gon guided the transport along the crowded air space surrounding the Senate.

"But it doesn't make sense," Obi-Wan said. "Her son died on another planet. And Didi has never met Senator S'orn."

"It doesn't make sense, true," Qui-Gon answered. "But it *has* to, somehow. We just have to figure out the connection."

Qui-Gon left the speeder in the Senate landing area. He strode into the Senate building. The usually crowded hallways were almost empty. Their footsteps echoed on the slate floor.

"What makes you think she'll be here so late?" Obi-Wan asked.

"Because her resignation was announced," Qui-Gon answered. "No doubt she had a busy afternoon. And she seems the kind of Senator to work late. Most of them leave as soon as Senate business has concluded." Qui-Gon paused, then remarked, "The Senate is not what it was. And it is getting worse. It has lost one idealist after another."

They made their way to the Senator's office. The outer office was dark, but Qui-Gon knocked on the inner door.

"Come in."

They entered. Only one light was on in the office. Senator S'orn sat in a chair, staring out at the bright Coruscant night. "Yes?" she asked without turning.

Qui-Gon closed the door behind them. "We regret having to disturb you."

She spun the chair around and sighed. "It has been a day of disturbances. I didn't expect my announcement to cause such a stir. I guess there's not much else going on."

"I do not wish to bring up something that is no doubt painful for you," Qui-Gon said gently. "But is your son's death the reason you are leaving?"

Senator S'orn's face changed. Her features hardened and her lips thinned. "Yes, I know why you are here. I should have given him up for Temple training. I was selfish."

"No," Qui-Gon said quickly. "Not at all. Many parents choose to keep a Force-sensitive child. There are many paths in life. You make the best choice you can for your child."

"So I chose to keep him with me, and that decision destroyed him," Senator S'orn said bitterly. "I chose a path that led to death."

"No, Ren chose his own path," Qui-Gon said firmly. "Senator S'orn, I do not know you. But I have known many Force-sensitive children. There is no more guarantee a Force-sensitive child will grow up to find happiness than one who does not have that ability. Many do not choose the Jedi path. Some flourish outside the Temple, and some do not. We are not here to question your decision or blame you."

"There is no need. I blame myself," Senator S'orn said bleakly. "Ever since I heard the news of Ren's death, I have been unable to focus, unable to do my job the way it needs to be done. I have managed to concentrate for only brief periods of time. What right have I to serve my people when I could not save my son?"

"I cannot answer that question for you," Qui-Gon said. "But perhaps you are right to take time apart from your life's journey. I have found such a time helpful, if you can look at your choices with forgiveness and calm."

"Forgiveness and calm seem very far away when your son is dead," Senator S'orn said in a choked voice. She spun her chair around so that her back was to them. When she turned again, she had composed herself. "But if you didn't come here to blame me, you certainly didn't come to counsel me, Qui-Gon Jinn. What is it that you are looking for?"

"I'm not quite sure," Qui-Gon said honestly. "Tell me something. When your data pad was stolen, why didn't you report the theft?"

She shrugged. "The chances of Senate security finding it were slim. My friend's data pad was stolen as well. Jenna didn't think it worthwhile to report. We were both too busy to bother."

Qui-Gon's watchful gaze turned alert. "Jenna?"

"Jenna Zan Arbor," Senator S'orn said. "She's a friend of mine, visiting the Senate for a conference. Surely you've heard of her. She's the foremost transgenic scientist in the galaxy, and a great humanitarian."

"Of course," Qui-Gon said. "You were together when the theft occurred?"

"It was in one of the hall cafés," Senator S'orn said. "We were having lunch."

Obi-Wan controlled his excitement. Something was about to break. He knew it. Fligh stole the data pad, and Jenna booked Didi's for an important dinner. Was this a connection that would lead them somewhere? As Qui-Gon had said earlier, it didn't make sense, but it *had* to.

"Was there anyone else in the café?"

Senator S'orn sighed. "Do you mean, was the

thief there? I assume so. Don't you think I've gone over this? The café was crowded. I didn't notice anyone suspicious."

"How about a tall, slender human male with one dark eye and one bright green eye?"

Senator S'orn looked startled. "Yes. But he couldn't be the thief. He's a Senatorial aide. Or at least he said so. We were discussing a dinner that Jenna was going to host for the other scientists attending the conference. He handed out a card for a restaurant nearby that he said was excellent. Jenna took the card. I had never heard of it, but Jenna said she would look into it."

Qui-Gon and Obi-Wan exchanged a glance.

"Was that the thief? Should I report him?" Senator S'orn asked.

Qui-Gon stood. "It would be to no purpose. He is dead. Thank you for your time, Senator."

Obi-Wan followed Qui-Gon from the office. "So we have a connection," he said. "Fligh and Didi to Jenna Zan Arbor and Senator S'orn."

"Not to mention to Ren S'orn," Qui-Gon said. "No doubt Jenna Zan Arbor knew about Senator S'orn's son."

"But I still don't see what it all means," Obi-Wan said, frustrated. "It's all so confusing."

"Ask yourself this question, Padawan. Who would benefit from Fligh's death? Or Didi's?"

"No one," Obi-Wan said. "Not now, anyway.

Unless there is something else on that data pad that we don't know about."

"Exactly," Qui-Gon said. "Either data pad — remember, we now know that Jenna Zan Arbor's data pad was stolen, too."

Obi-Wan nodded. "I have a feeling I know where we're heading next."

"Yes," Qui-Gon said. "To see Jenna Zan Arbor."

CHAPTER 12

Obi-Wan stood uneasily in the lobby of the luxury hotel. He had been in palaces and grand houses before. He had seen luxurious surroundings, thick carpets, fine metals, ornately carved furniture. He had observed without feeling part of it, as a Jedi should. He had never felt awkward, even in the palace of a queen.

But here he felt differently. The walls were of a white polished stone with veins of pinkish gold. The floor under his feet was black hard stone, polished to a high sheen. He was afraid to sit on the plush sofas and chairs. He suddenly noticed the stains of his dessert on his tunic.

The rich swirled around him, coming to and fro from the many restaurants off the lobby, or picking up mail and keys. Their eyes slid past him, as if he was not worth their notice. Their voices were low and hushed, unlike the busy chatter on the crowded streets.

As usual, Qui-Gon looked perfectly at ease. He walked to the desk and asked the clerk to ring Jenna Zan Arbor's room.

The clerk spoke into a private comlink headpiece and listened for a moment. "You may go up," he said. Then he directed them to the turbolift that would take them to the seventy-seventh floor.

Obi-Wan followed Qui-Gon into a large lift tube lined with a rosy stone that made him feel as though he were in the center of a flower. The tube doors opened, and he stepped out onto a thick, cushioned carpet.

Jenna Zan Arbor waited in the doorway of her suite. She was dressed in a septsilk robe of deep blue that hung stiffly to her feet. Her blond hair was again twisted in an elaborate style and wound through with multicolored fabric.

Qui-Gon bowed. "Thank you for seeing us. I am Qui-Gon Jinn and this is Obi-Wan Kenobi."

She returned the bow. "Jenna Zan Arbor. I'm honored to greet the Jedi." She gave them another look. "But you were at the café."

"We are friends of Astri and Didi Oddo," Qui-Gon said.

Jenna Zan Arbor looked a little less welcoming. She turned and led them into a vast room with the same polished black stone floor as the lobby. Plush white sofas were arranged in two seating areas, one intimate and one grand. Gauzy white draperies hung at the floor-to-ceiling windows and pooled on the floor. Outside, the lights of the passing traffic were like traveling stars through a fine mist.

Jenna Zan Arbor ushered them to the most intimate grouping. Obi-Wan sat down and immediately sank into the cushions. He tried to sit erect but found himself slipping backward.

Zan Arbor waved her hand at the room. "I don't feel comfortable with all this. But the conference is paying for it. I'm used to a more . . . practical environment. I spend most of my time in my lab." She turned luminous gray eyes to them. "What can I do for you?"

"We are investigating a murder," Qui-Gon said. "Someone you spoke with at the Senate. His name was Fligh. He posed as a Senatorial aide and gave you a card for Didi's restaurant —"

"Of course, I remember," Zan Arbor said immediately. "He had one green eye. He praised the food and atmosphere of this place. I don't know Coruscant very well, so I followed up on the tip."

"Why did you leave the café so abruptly tonight?" Qui-Gon asked.

The scientist gave a low laugh. "Because my guests were miserable. It was not what I had been led to expect. I know that sounds snobbish, but I was trying to make a good impression. The conference has a number of grants for scientific projects. I need funding." She shrugged slender shoulders. "So we came back here and the hotel accommodated us." She paused. "But why should my dinner have anything to do with this person's death?"

Instead of answering, Qui-Gon asked another question. "You are friends with Senator S'orn?"

"Yes."

"And you know that her son died, and how he died, I presume," Qui-Gon said.

Zan Arbor nodded, but a frosty look took over her warm gaze. "Of course I do. I hardly think it's your business. That was a great tragedy for Uta."

"Not for you, though," Qui-Gon stated.

She gave him a hard look. "No. I was sorry for my friend, but it was not a personal tragedy. What are you implying?"

"Nothing at all," Qui-Gon said easily. "We are just investigating. Could I have a list of the guests at your dinner?"

"Why?" Zan Arbor asked, irritation now coloring her even tone.

"Because someone attacked the owner and

his daughter after your party left," Qui-Gon answered. "I don't think it's necessary, but later it might help if we could question them."

"I hardly think . . ." Zan Arbor's irritated tone ended in a shrug. "Why not. I have nothing to hide." She crossed to a desk and scrawled some names on a durasheet, then handed it to Obi-Wan. He tucked it in his tunic.

She sat down again. "Can I ask you what Ren S'orn's murder has to do with this Fligh person, or the attack at the café?"

"Maybe nothing at all," Qui-Gon said.

The scientist's gaze was cool. "I think I'm beginning to understand. You don't want information from me. You think I may be involved."

"I did not mean to imply that," Qui-Gon said.

"Yet here you are," she pointed out crisply. "I assume you know who I am."

Qui-Gon nodded.

"I'm not accustomed to someone coming to my private quarters and linking me to a murder. Murder is not a topic that is familiar to me. I live in the world of transgenic research. So you must forgive me if I'm a little confused and upset."

"Of course," Qui-Gon said. "Murder is an upsetting topic."

Zan Arbor gave a brief smile. "Especially for

the victim. Let's finish this. What else do you need to know?"

"Why didn't you report the theft of your data pad?" Qui-Gon asked. "You must have been upset about it."

"I was not upset. I have backup of all my files on data cards."

"Uta S'orn was upset," Qui-Gon said.

"She had a reason to be," Zan Arbor answered, an edge to her voice. "She had private information on that data pad. She was forced to resign before pushing through an important piece of legislation."

"Do you happen to know what that is?" Obi-Wan asked. He had been content to watch Qui-Gon ask the questions. But the legislation had come up before, and he was curious to know what it was.

"Yes. Uta told me all about it. I wasn't that interested, frankly. My head is full of science. But apparently she was trying to put together a coalition of planets to join together to fight some sort of black market tech gang. She probably had all the votes she needed. But her resignation changed that. Without her to hold the alliance together, things will probably fall apart. Are we through?"

Obi-Wan did not look at Qui-Gon, but elation

surged through him. This was a crucial clue. The Tech Raiders had a reason to want to discredit Senator S'orn. She was trying to pass a law that could lead to their destruction. Helb knew both Fligh and Didi. Here was the link. No doubt Helb had recruited Fligh to steal the Senator's data pad. Fligh had gone further and stolen the scientist's; most likely for his own profit. All they had to do now was figure out how Didi was involved.

So Senator S'orn and Jenna Zan Arbor were just what they appeared to be: two powerful women who were simply victims of petty theft.

He did not need to glance at his Master to know that Qui-Gon had reached the same conclusions.

"We're through," Qui-Gon said.

Obi-Wan felt a thrill as they left the hotel suite and entered the turbolift.

"This is it," he said. "This is the connection we've been looking for. We're close to solving the mystery."

"Perhaps," Qui-Gon said. "We need to talk to Helb again, that is certain."

"Tomorrow we'll solve the mystery, and Didi and Astri can come home," Obi-Wan said. "If we confront the Tech Raiders with what we know, they'll have to recall the bounty hunter. It's got to be them, doesn't it? They wanted to prevent that legislation from going through. Somehow Fligh got Didi mixed up in it. Maybe they hoped to sell both data pads to some other party. That would definitely anger Helb."

The lift tube doors opened and they walked out into the grand lobby. The floor-to-ceiling windows revealed the black night outside.

"It's too late to find Helb now," Qui-Gon said. "Let's return to the Temple. We both need sleep."

Outside the side door was a large landing platform for the many vehicles of the guests of the hotel. Qui-Gon had left their speeder close to the door so that they would be able to leave quickly, but now a row of other vehicles had blocked it in.

He signaled to the parking clerk. "Can you move those other vehicles?"

"Right away, sir," the young boy replied. He jumped into the first speeder to move it.

Qui-Gon and Obi-Wan headed toward their own vehicle. Qui-Gon slipped into the driver's seat. Obi-Wan had a bit more trouble getting into the passenger side. The speeder was jammed up next to another. He had to swing one leg up and over in order to enter.

He was in the middle of the maneuver when he felt a sudden jolt send him flying backward. The clerk had backed his speeder into the one behind. Obi-Wan slid backward on the smooth metal. Behind him was the railing. Past that was only the empty air.

"Hey, you —" Qui-Gon suddenly vaulted out of the driver's seat, alert to danger.

He was too late. The clerk hit the speeder behind his again, and the Jedi's speeder jolted backward. Obi-Wan felt himself slide off the back end of the speeder. He was thrown over the railing, straight into space.

CHAPTER 13

Everything had happened so fast, but Obi-Wan's extraordinary reflexes gave him a second to plan. It was enough. As he shot over the railing, he was already accessing his liquid cable launcher. He aimed it at the platform edge. It engaged.

The line played out, and he swung in empty space. It was an eerie feeling. A cruiser zoomed by him, its driver surprised to see a boy dangling in the middle of a space lane.

Obi-Wan felt sweat trickle down his flanks. He retracted the launcher, and it carried him up to the platform level. Qui-Gon was waiting.

"That was fast thinking, Obi-Wan," Qui-Gon said, relieved and agitated. "Your reflexes did not fail you. I should have been more alert."

"Where is the parking clerk?" Obi-Wan asked.

"Took off in the speeder," Qui-Gon said grimly.

"Do you think the bounty hunter bribed him?"

"I think the boy *was* the bounty hunter," Qui-Gon said. "We will not make that mistake again." He felt lightheaded with relief and realized that fatigue had set in at last. "Come. We can't do any more tonight. We need to rest. At least we know the bounty hunter is still on Coruscant and is not tracking Didi and Astri."

By the time they reached the Temple, Obi-Wan's steps were dragging. His close call had cost him. Qui-Gon was glad to send him to his quarters.

Back in his own quarters, Qui-Gon lay on his sleep couch in the darkness. He wished for rest, but even a Jedi could not summon sleep when the mind was active.

She had deceived him again. She had nearly killed Obi-Wan. She was thinking faster than he was. It was because his preoccupation with the *whys* of the investigation was leading him to be less vigilant. He had been more worried about Didi than about his own Padawan.

Qui-Gon thought back to the interview with Jenna Zan Arbor. Obi-Wan was right. It made sense that the Tech Raiders would want to steal Senator S'orn's data pad. No doubt they had engaged Fligh for the task. It was in Fligh's character to hold out on them. And it was possible that Fligh had concealed the data pad within the café, involving Didi. Perhaps he'd tried to retrieve it and that was why he'd been killed.

Qui-Gon stared at the ceiling. Logic told him that this scenario made sense. Why couldn't he sleep?

It was because the killing of Fligh did not seem like the job of a criminal gang like the Tech Raiders. They did not need to disguise their work, to send the Coruscant security forces on the wrong path. They arrogantly thought themselves too big to care about a local investigation.

No, Fligh's murder still did not make sense. That indicated to Qui-Gon that it was about emotion, not logic.

He thought back to Senator S'orn. He had glimpsed the despair and bitterness deep within her. Such emotions could drive someone to evil, certainly.

Jenna Zan Arbor appeared to have nothing to hide. Yet it still bothered him that she'd shown up at Didi's Café. True, she didn't know Coruscant, but her friend did. She could have asked for a recommendation from Uta S'orn. Why did she take the advice of a stranger?

Murder is an upsetting topic.

Especially for the victim.

There was something cold in the way Jenna Zan Arbor had smiled when she made that light remark. Her smile was keeping Qui-Gon awake.

And the vision of Obi-Wan shooting over that railing into deep space while he scrambled to get to him. And the knowledge that the bounty hunter would likely return to Didi and Astri's trail.

Yes, he had much on his mind.

He reached out to the night. He pulled the darkness around himself. He drew long slow breaths. He could do nothing tonight. His worry about Didi and Astri would simmer inside him, would flare to life again in the morning. Until then, he would sleep.

The next morning, Helb was nowhere to be found.

"This is suspicious," Obi-Wan said. "No doubt he knows that we are on to him."

Qui-Gon had decided not to share his feeling that the Tech Raiders were not responsible for Fligh's death. He had only cloudy doubts and vague feelings to report; he wanted more concrete evidence.

And Helb knew more than he was telling. That was certain.

"There is only one place left he can be," Qui-

Gon said. "Vandor-3. He's got to be at the base. We should get answers there."

Vandor-3 was a neighboring satellite planet of Coruscant. Luckily Qui-Gon had taken a cruiser from the Temple landing platform, just in case they needed to travel beyond Coruscant's atmosphere. It was a short journey to Vandor-3.

They hovered outside the base's air space until they were given clearance to land. Qui-Gon saw the landing platform below, in the midst of what looked like a salvage yard. He eased the cruiser down between a maintenance hauler and a sea of swoops.

As soon as they released the loading ramp and exited, they were assaulted by noise. Workers and droids were everywhere, cutting metal, soldering circuits, dragging materials, operating gravsleds. Voices were raised in argument over the loud buzzing of hydraulic metal cutters, macrofusers, and hydrospanners. Enormous repulsorlift engines hung over their heads on a system of straps and pulleys. Speeder parts, circuit boards, boosters, converters, and other parts Obi-Wan did not recognize were divided into various piles.

"This is quite an operation," Qui-Gon said as they edged their way past a starship, its engine parts laid out on the floor.

"Watch out for that acceleration compensator!" a voice bellowed.

Obi-Wan took a quick step sideways to avoid the equipment as Helb barreled toward them, his orange eyes sparking irritation.

"I'm guessing you didn't come here for a deal on speeder parts," he yelled over the noise.

"Just information," Qui-Gon yelled back.

"Well, you're in the way here. Follow me."

The Jedi followed Helb into a quieter corner of the yard. A small shed made out of salvaged materials stood against a durasteel fence. Helb pushed the door open.

Inside, the din dulled to a dim roar.

"I'd ask you to sit, but you're leaving," Helb snapped. "I thought I made it clear that I've told you all I know."

"I don't think you have," Qui-Gon said. "I think you've left something out. I think your gang hired Fligh to steal Senator S'orn's data pad. Most likely Fligh had to agree to do it because he owed you money."

Helb didn't say anything. He crossed his arms.

"Maybe Fligh didn't turn over the data pad. Maybe he thought he could get more money out of you," Qui-Gon guessed, watching Helb carefully. "Maybe that's why you put the death mark on his head. You suspected he had given the data pad to Didi."

"Listen, I'm not pretending to be overflowing with goodness, Jedi," Helb said. "I'd sell out my brother for money. But we didn't put a death mark on Fligh. Now get out of here before I call the security droids."

Qui-Gon didn't move. He put one hand on his lightsaber hilt. Obi-Wan did the same.

Helb shifted uncomfortably. "Look, we don't want to get on the wrong side of the Jedi."

"Then tell us the truth, and we will go," Qui-Gon said.

"All right, all right. Yes, we did get Fligh to steal the data pad. The bantha-brain stole the wrong one! He should have taken her official data pad, not the one with her personal correspondence. But it worked out fine, because we didn't know she was planning to resign. We got what we wanted anyway. Her legislation is dead. Why would we put a death mark on Fligh? Sure, he was a weasel, but he was a valuable weasel. Sent a lot of clients our way."

"Fligh stole two data pads that day," Qui-Gon said. "Do you know what happened to the other one?"

Helb shrugged. "Probably sold it, or gave it to someone he owed money to."

Obi-Wan and Qui-Gon exchanged a glance. "Didi," Obi-Wan murmured.

"Maybe," Helb said, overhearing him. "I'm sure Fligh owed Didi, too. Didi is the shrewdest sabacc player around. We all played that game of sabacc together. I lost to Didi, too. None of us could pay off Didi that day, but he let us slide. I didn't pay him off until a few days later. Luckily I had something to trade with."

"What did you trade?" Qui-Gon asked.

"I passed along this hideout I had in the Cascardi Mountains," Helb said. "I never would have used it, anyway. I won it in a game of chance off some old fool wrapped in a pile of cloaks at the Splendor. As a matter of fact, it was the day I met the two of you —"

Helb didn't get a chance to finish his sentence.

The two Jedi were gone.

CHAPTER 14

From above, the house in the Cascardi Mountains looked quiet. It was a white, three-story structure built into the mountainside that blended in with the snow. They could see Didi's cruiser parked on the small landing platform that was off the second floor. There was no sign of Didi and Astri.

Qui-Gon landed their cruiser next to Didi's. They climbed out and approached the door with caution. They kept their lightsabers in their hands but not activated. This time, they would be prepared.

Qui-Gon concentrated, listening for movement, for anything out of the ordinary. Obi-Wan was tense beside him. He trusted the boy's instincts. "What do you think?" he asked quietly.

"I'm not feeling anything clearly," Obi-Wan said. "Yet something is wrong. As though Didi and Astri are not in danger, but danger is here."

Qui-Gon nodded. "I feel that, too. She has lured them here. No wonder she remained on Coruscant and trailed us. She did not have to track Didi and Astri. She knew where they were. The sooner we get them away from here, the better."

A window slid open above them, and Didi popped his head out. Relief creased his features. "It's you, thank the moons and stars. I'll activate the door for you. I am so very glad to see you."

A moment later the door slid open. Qui-Gon and Obi-Wan walked inside and were met by Didi as he hurried down a curving ramp from upstairs.

"Is everything all right?" Qui-Gon asked, clipping his lightsaber back onto his utility belt.

Didi nodded. "I suppose. At first we were glad to be here. We felt safe. The place is so remote and hidden. But now the isolation is getting on our nerves. I think we would feel safer back on Coruscant."

"Where is Astri?" Obi-Wan asked.

"Here." Astri appeared from the other room. "I am so happy to see you both. The hours have been very long."

"No sign of trouble?" Qui-Gon asked. "Nothing out of the ordinary?"

"Nothing," Didi said.

"We keep a lookout," Astri said. "We watch out the windows for cruisers. We saw you approach. We weren't sure who it was." She tapped a blaster strapped to her hip. "I was ready."

"Have you ever used a blaster before, Astri?" Qui-Gon asked cautiously.

"How hard could it be?" Astri said. "Point and shoot. Easy as making a meal."

After having seen her kitchen, Qui-Gon was not sure he trusted Astri's shooting. "I'll give you a lesson in a moment," he told her. "How about you, Didi? Do you have a weapon?"

"Are you serious?" Didi shook his head. "I don't like Astri having one, either. How do you think I managed to stay out of trouble all these years?"

"We must speak to you both seriously," Qui-Gon said. "You must tell us the truth. Your safety depends on it."

"But you said we were safe here," Didi said nervously.

Qui-Gon shook his head. "I did not. This only bought us time. I'm afraid time has run out."

"What do you need to know?" Astri asked.

Qui-Gon turned to Didi. "Fligh stole two data pads. We think one of them is the key to your problem. He must have given one to you, Didi. Did he leave a case, or a bin, or anything with you? Could he have hidden something when your back was turned?"

"I would never turn my back on Fligh," Didi said. "You have asked me this already, my friend. I give you the same answer. Fligh gave me nothing."

Obi-Wan noticed a flush spread over Astri's cheeks.

"What about you, Astri?" he asked.

She glanced at her father. "Well. Sometimes I used Fligh for more than sweeping."

"You used Fligh?" Didi asked, incredulous. "After you told me I should not associate with him?"

Astri looked uncomfortable. "We were not getting enough business. I'd spent so much money on the café. If it closed you'd never let me forget it. And I knew that Fligh hung around the Senate. I paid him to pass along tips to me about which Senators would be hosting important dinners. Then I could have a head start and bid on the job. Recently Fligh came to me with two pieces of information: one, that someone might throw Senator S'orn a going-away party soon, and two, that Jenna Zan Arbor was hosting a testimonial dinner. I paid him for both tips."

"You paid him for information? Ha!" Didi

cried. "I am not the only one in this family to stretch the truth a bit!"

"This isn't the time to reproach Astri," Qui-Gon said sternly.

"I am not reproaching! I am *congratulating*," Didi insisted.

Astri's cheeks were pink. "Anyway, Fligh gave me a data pad for safekeeping. He told me he had just traded for it. He asked me to keep it for him. I was in the middle of something, so I stuck it in one of the ovens. The oven was broken," she added hastily. "To tell you the truth, I forgot about it until the night we left."

"Where is it now?" Qui-Gon asked urgently.

"Here," Astri said. "I brought it with us. My data pad was smashed, so I thought I'd use this one."

She reached over to a nearby table and handed it to Qui-Gon. "I haven't had a chance to see what's on it yet."

Qui-Gon quickly accessed the files on the data pad. A strange code streamed across the screen.

"The files are all coded," he mused.

"They must be Jenna Zan Arbor's," Obi-Wan said, looking over his shoulder. "These are probably formulas."

"Yes. Let me send it to Tahl. She can take it to

our code experts." Qui-Gon jacked into the data pad and transferred the files to his own com-link. He then contacted Tahl.

"Sure, send it along," Tahl said. "I'll get right on it and contact you as soon as we break it."

"This is high priority," Qui-Gon told her. He switched off the connection. "I don't think we should wait. I have several destinations in mind. There are contacts who can hide you," he told Didi and Astri.

"I won't mind leaving this place," Astri said with a shiver. "It's awfully lonely. Just us and the lonesome wind. The caretaker told us there's no one here at this time of year. At first we thought this an advantage."

Obi-Wan and Qui-Gon froze.

"Caretaker?" Qui-Gon asked.

"She came with the place," Didi said. "Relax, Qui-Gon. She's at least a hundred years old."

"Where is she?" Qui-Gon asked, his hand on his lightsaber.

Astri looked puzzled. "She brings provisions once a day. She's not here now."

Qui-Gon's uneasy feeling changed to alarm.

Simultaneously, the two Jedi activated their lightsabers.

"Let's get to the cruiser," Qui-Gon said.

"But our things —" Astri began.

"Leave them."

They started toward the door, but it was too late. At that moment, durasteel coverings on the windows slid down with a clang. They heard the harsh sound of locks snapping throughout the house. The snug hideaway had turned into a prison.

They were trapped. And Qui-Gon had no doubt that the bounty hunter was in the house with them.

CHAPTER 15

"What's going on?" Didi whispered.

"Where is the lighting console?" Qui-Gon asked Didi.

"Over there." Didi pointed to a console that was mounted on a table.

Qui-Gon strode over and powered down all the lights. Darkness dropped like a curtain. Obi-Wan could not see a thing, but he waited, knowing his eyes would adjust.

"Remember how she fought last time, Padawan," Qui-Gon said to him in a murmur. "Her strategy is to attack those we defend in order to keep us busy. Expect her to move in their direction first. Watch her shoulders to tell you which way she will move."

"I have the data pad, Qui-Gon," Astri whispered. "It's in my tunic."

"Keep it safe," Qui-Gon whispered back. "We don't need it anymore, but it is our insurance. If the bounty hunter thinks we can tell her where it is, she won't kill us."

"Ah, reassuring news," Didi said. His voice shook with terror.

"Stay between us," Qui-Gon instructed Didi and Astri. "We can't protect you if you stray. We're going to cut through those window shields."

They moved forward with Astri and Didi between them. Obi-Wan's vision had adjusted and he kept his eyes moving around the room, waiting for a shadow to move and materialize into the bounty hunter.

But even he was not prepared for how fast she struck. The laser whip came out of nowhere, spiraling in the air toward Astri. Qui-Gon leaped forward, lightsaber already slashing downward. It collided with the whip. A harsh buzzing sound rose from the contact.

The whip curled back and struck again, this time toward Didi. Obi-Wan was prepared, stepping into his left-to-right sweep. The whip wrapped around his lightsaber and smoked before uncurling and flying backward. The lightsaber could not cut it.

He could see her now. At least he could see the shape of her body. He could not see her eyes. She was dressed all in black; it was hard to track her as she moved. Only the slight gleam of her boots and armor told him where she was heading. She did not make a sound.

The whip unfurled again, dancing over their heads as though it were a living thing. Qui-Gon and Obi-Wan kept their lightsabers moving, twirling them above their heads to fend off the lethal whip. All the while Qui-Gon pressed steadily forward.

Suddenly Astri began to fire her blaster. Her shots went widely off the mark, peppering the durasteel over the windows. The blasts ricocheted back toward them. Obi-Wan and Qui-Gon had to move quickly to deflect them. In the meantime, the whip snaked out again and knocked the blaster from Astri's hand. It skittered across the floor.

Qui-Gon and Obi-Wan kept moving toward the windows. The bounty hunter realized their objective and sprang forward, somersaulting in a blur toward them. Her move ended in a sharp kick, close enough to land a glancing blow at Astri's ribs. A slight clang resulted from the sole of her boot hitting Astri's tunic. Obi-Wan saw the knowledge in the bounty hunter's face. She knew that Astri had the data pad.

Pushing Astri behind him, Qui-Gon launched an attack at the bounty hunter. She kept the whip moving in a blur of light. Suddenly she flipped backward in a series of fast moves, eluding the Jedi. She was still between them and the windows. In a quick reversal of strategy, Qui-Gon pushed Astri and Didi up the ramp.

"Run," he directed.

The bounty hunter was still flipping over, thinking she needed to put distance between herself and the Jedi. She would need time to find her feet and reverse again to face them.

"Run, Padawan," Qui-Gon said.

Obi-Wan dashed up the ramp. He guessed what Qui-Gon was thinking. If they could get to the windows above, they could cut through the durasteel. From there it would be an easy drop to the landing platform. He heard Qui-Gon hit the ramp behind him.

As they reached the upper level, their keen hearing told them that the bounty hunter was in fast pursuit. Quickly, Qui-Gon opened a shelving unit with various cubbyholes that ran along the wall with the windows.

"Don't come out until I get you," he told Didi and Astri, herding them inside.

He shut the doors after them and motioned to Obi-Wan to get to work on the durasteel-blocked windows. Then he rushed forward to meet the bounty hunter as she ran up the curving ramp. She came into sight in seconds but instead of meeting Qui-Gon she gave a leap in the air. She grabbed onto the system of conduit pipes near the ceiling and used her momentum to fly over Qui-Gon's head, straight at Obi-Wan.

Obi-Wan kicked out with one leg as he tried to turn to meet the attack. He had been in an awkward position, just beginning to cut through the durasteel with his lightsaber. He felt the studded spikes on the end of the whip catch his leg as he turned. The pain seared him, but he kept moving, raising his lightsaber to meet the flashing whip.

Without Astri and Didi to defend, the Jedi were now free to attack. They moved toward the bounty hunter as one unit, lightsabers whirling and arcing, anticipating her moves and the striking, curling whip.

Obi-Wan remembered Qui-Gon's directive to watch the bounty hunter's shoulders. Her footwork was fast but she had a tendency to lean into her moves.

She began to retreat backward, though the action of her whip did not falter. In the glow of the lightsabers and whip, he could read an expression on her face: sheer rage. No doubt she had never fought Jedi like this before.

When at last she stood at the edge of the curving ramp, Obi-Wan made a bold move. He copied her action, leaping up to grab onto the conduit pipes overhead, then as the whip snaked and curled around him, drove into her with both feet.

She let out a surprised sound as she flew back, high above the ramp. She landed with a solid thud, then continued to skid down the ramp. She tried to stop her descent but the smooth stone was slippery. Her leg twisted underneath her and her head hit the stone wall with another sickening thud.

She lay still.

"Hurry, Padawan." Qui-Gon strode to the windows. Together with Obi-Wan he cut through the durasteel. It peeled back, leaving an opening big enough for them to get through.

Qui-Gon threw open the cubbyhole doors. Quickly, Obi-Wan helped Didi and Astri to the window ledge.

"You'll have to carry Astri," Qui-Gon told him. "I'll take Didi."

Without pausing to reply, Obi-Wan swept up the slender Astri in his arms. Qui-Gon picked up plump Didi with the same ease. Then they leaped into the air and landed softly on the ground below.

Qui-Gon jumped into the pilot seat of their cruiser. He fired up the engine. Red warning lights flashed, and there was no answering surge of power.

"She tampered with it," he said tersely.

"Let's try ours," Didi suggested, already running toward his own cruiser.

They followed, but Qui-Gon and Obi-Wan were not surprised when Didi's cruiser would not operate.

"She has to have transport nearby. If we —" Qui-Gon began, but his words were drowned out by a piercing, animallike cry.

For a moment, the light was blocked out as the bounty hunter threw herself out the window above. Her lips were curled back in a snarl.

She landed on one leg, whip flashing, and went straight for Obi-Wan.

CHAPTER 16

Qui-Gon sprang forward to place himself between Obi-Wan and the bounty hunter as Didi and Astri leaped back to get out of his way. Obi-Wan used the opportunity to quickly scan the mountainside. It was crucial that they locate some form of transport. They had to get Didi and Astri away, even if he and Qui-Gon had to hold off the bounty hunter long enough for Didi and Astri to take off.

At first he couldn't distinguish anything. The snow was thick and blindingly white, dotted with boulders and crags. The sun bounced off the snow, hurting his eyes.

He had only seconds. Obi-Wan drew the Force around him, connecting him to everything he saw, from the craggy peaks and rocks to the fresh, dense snow.

He only saw a slight irregularity in the surface of the snow hundreds of meters below him.

Then he snapped his gaze back. It was a small cruiser. It was white, and it nestled in the snow, but he made out its outlines.

"Down there," Obi-Wan told Didi and Astri crisply as Qui-Gon's lightsaber tangled with the bounty hunter's whip. "Below that crag."

"I see it," Astri said.

"Go," Obi-Wan urged, already spinning to cover Qui-Gon's flank. "Don't wait for us!"

Didi and Astri stepped off the landing platform onto the snow. They sank into the snow up to their knees. They pushed through, making their way slowly across the side of the mountain. Drifts alternated with patches of ice, but they pushed on.

The bounty hunter redoubled her efforts, suddenly launching an offensive that sent Qui-Gon and Obi-Wan back against the edge of the landing platform. She had grabbed Astri's blaster and let loose a stream of fire from one hand while the other expertly plied her whip.

Their lightsabers were a blur as they fought off the frenzied attack. She pushed her advantage, and they stepped off the landing platform into the snow.

Now their footing was uneven. Obi-Wan expected an attack, but the bounty hunter changed her tactics. Instead of pressing on, she turned her back and raced to the other end of the landing platform.

She poised on the edge and pressed a device in her utility belt. A thin material skin shot out from her shoulders and thighs, creating a cradle around her. She leaped into the air and came down on the snow on her back. Then she dug her heels into the snow and Obi-Wan could see that there were now spikes protruding from her boot soles.

"She is prepared, as usual," Qui-Gon said.

She pushed herself off and flew down the mountain in the improvised sled, gaining speed as she went.

"She's going to come at Didi and Astri from below," Obi-Wan said. "She'll be between them and the transport."

"Exactly. We must reach them first."

Didi and Astri had made some progress. Though the footing was treacherous, desperation had fueled their speed. They had not seen the bounty hunter yet.

Obi-Wan and Qui-Gon hurried down the steep incline in their direction, carefully negotiating the ice and drifts. Obi-Wan glanced down the mountain at the bounty hunter. He could not imagine how she would manage to stop her descent. But as she slid, she unfurled her whip.

With an expert flick, the whip arced in the sky and looped around a craggy boulder. As the whip went taut, she dug her heels into the snow. Her treacherous slide was halted. She rolled to her side and sprang up, then detached the sled and began to race across the mountainside.

She made good progress as she moved across and up the face of the slope. Qui-Gon called out to Didi and Astri, alerting them to the fact that their enemy was now below them.

They hesitated, not knowing which way to go. Holding each other, they stood in the shadow of a crag. If they continued their descent, they would walk straight into the bounty hunter. The crag was too steep to climb.

Didi looked over at Qui-Gon helplessly.

"Stay there!" Qui-Gon shouted as he pushed through a drift. "We will come to you."

Obi-Wan wasn't worried. They were closer to Didi and Astri than the bounty hunter was. They would be able to reach them before she did, he had no doubt.

They were almost to the pair when the bounty hunter cracked her whip and sent it flying toward Astri. It lengthened farther than they had ever seen it go, growing longer and longer as it sailed through the air. It was not in laser mode, so it did not cut her. Instead, it whipped around her ankle. Didi desperately tried to hold on, but Astri was yanked off her feet and slid down the mountain, straight at the bounty hunter. At the same time, the bounty hunter reached down to her holster, withdrew a blaster, and shot Didi. He fell softly, silently, into the snow.

"She knows Astri has the data pad," Qui-Gon said tersely. "See to Didi. I have an idea."

Qui-Gon activated his lightsaber again. He kept it in front of him, sweeping the snow with each stride to cut a narrow path through it. The ice melted in seconds, and he was able to hit firm ground. He made fast progress down the mountain. But not fast enough.

Obi-Wan used the same technique to get to Didi. He fervently hoped he was still alive. He fell to his knees by Didi's side and reached for the emergency medpac on his belt. He saw the spreading stain of blood on Didi's tunic and ripped it open. He quickly poured bacta into the wound.

Didi's eyes fluttered open. Despair pooled in his deep brown gaze. "Astri," he murmured.

Obi-Wan turned. Qui-Gon had not yet reached the bounty hunter, but Astri had. She lay at their enemy's feet. The bounty hunter had one booted foot on her chest. She reached down for the data pad, which had slipped out of Astri's tunic. Astri held the data pad in a death-grip. The bounty hunter set the whip to laser mode and it glowed red.

Qui-Gon was too far away to stop her.

"Astri," Didi moaned.

Obi-Wan summoned the Force. He felt the power in his muscles as he leaped from Didi's side onto the crag. He scrambled to the top in seconds. Then he bent his knees and gathered power for the spring. He leaped high in the air, so high that the bounty hunter sensed his presence in the sky and looked up, confused. She only had time to raise her arm back before Obi-Wan, in the same maneuver he had used in the house, came straight at her, feet first. He hit both of her shoulders with a mighty blow that sent her backward onto the snow. Obi-Wan landed in the snow, his feet planted on either side of her body, his lightsaber raised.

"Enough," he said.

She lay rigid, but he felt a flicker of movement in her right hand. He saw the glint of a vibro-blade. Moving only her fingers, she flicked it with expert aim toward Astri.

Obi-Wan's blow with the lightsaber was only a split second too late. It grazed the bounty hunter's fingers in a searing wound. At the same time he leaped backward, twisting in midair to try to catch the blade with his other hand. He used his Jedi reflexes to slow time down, allowing him to eye exactly where to grab it. The hilt thudded into his hand.

The bounty hunter stuck her wounded fingers in the snow for an instant. Her teeth sank into her lower lip.

The pain must have been terrible. She spoke for the first time. Her eyes blazed hatred at Obi-Wan. "You . . . will . . . pay."

Suddenly a lunge line shot out from her utility belt. It had a homing beacon to her cruiser, attaching itself to it and yanking her backward. Her body bounced across the ice. It must have been excruciatingly painful.

"Stay with them," Qui-Gon directed, and took off after her.

Obi-Wan watched as Qui-Gon gained on the bounty hunter. She scrambled into her cruiser. The engines fired and the loading ramp began to close as Qui-Gon gave a great leap and landed.

Horrified, Obi-Wan saw the flash of blaster fire. Qui-Gon staggered.

"Master!" Obi-Wan screamed.

Qui-Gon fell backward into the bowels of the ship. The ramp retracted. The ship rose in the air and shot away into the upper atmosphere.

Obi-Wan could hear as if for the first time the wind whispering along the surface of the snow. Astri raggedly breathed behind him. The echo of his own anguished cry reverberated off the mountain as he watched the ship disappear.

Had Qui-Gon been captured by the bounty hunter, or had he captured her? Was he mortally wounded? Was he alive — or dead?

The anguish of not knowing made Obi-Wan want to crash to his knees. But there were wounded he had to care for. Qui-Gon had told him to stay.

"Don't lose heart, Qui-Gon," he whispered. "I'll find you. Hold on."

He would find a way to bring back his Master.

Look for

JEDI APPRENTICE

The Evil Experiment

He heard sound, but it was only a rush of white noise. His eyes were open, but he could only see vapor. He was wet, but he was not in water. Since he was not able to trust his sight or hearing, Qui-Gon Jinn decided to focus on the pain.

He tracked its location and measured its quality. It was on the left side of his chest, above his heart, and ran up to his shoulder. It wasn't a white-hot pain, but a steady burning ache, as deep as muscle and bone.

It told him he was alive.

He tried to move his right arm. The slight contraction of muscle, the effort required, seemed enormous. He hit something smooth with his fingers. He followed it slowly, tracing it up, then down. He moved his other arm and reached out his hand. Again, he met a solid wall. It was all around him. He realized that he was trapped.

A jolt of panic raced through him as he realized that he did not remember why he was here.

Qui-Gon allowed it to exist and then watched it go. He breathed deeply. He was a Jedi Knight. His lightsaber was gone as well as his utility belt, but he still had the Force.

He was not alone.

As he breathed, Qui-Gon brought his mind to stillness. He told himself that his memory would return. He would not strain for it. He did not need it to live in the present moment.

He concentrated on his surroundings. Slowly he realized that he was in a transparent chamber. The reason he felt dizzy and strange was that he hung suspended, upside down. A cloudy gas surrounded him. Somehow it kept him floating in the tank. He could not see clearly through the vapor to the outside. He shifted, hoping to change position, and pain shot down his shoulder to his side. Blaster wounds were tricky. You thought the flesh was knitting, and then your wound told you otherwise if you tried too much, too soon . .

Blaster wound.

Memories flooded back.

He had been on a mountainside with his Padawan, Obi-Wan Kenobi. They were trying to protect his friend Didi Oddo and Didi's Daughter, Astri. The bounty hunter had shot Didi, and he had falled —

Didi!

The Early Adventures of
Obi-Wan Kenobi and Qui-Gon Jinn

STAR WARS®

JEDI APPRENTICE

Visit us at www.scholastic.com

COME OUT OF THE DARKNESS.

SEVENTH TOWER™

BOOK THREE

TAL AND MILLA ARE ON A QUEST IN THE
DREAM WORLD AENIR, WHERE IMPOSSIBLE
THINGS HAPPEN ALL THE TIME AND DANGER
HAUNTS EVERY MOMENT. TAL MUST FIND THE
ONE THING THAT CAN SAVE HIS FAMILY AND
HIS WORLD — BUT TO DO SO HE MIGHT HAVE TO
PAY AN UNTHINKABLE PRICE.

AVAILABLE IN BOOKSTORES DECEMBER 2000

VISIT US ONLINE AT

WWW.THESEVENTHTOWER.COM